"Marcus," she said, simply for lack of anything else. **"Did you forget something?"**

"Yes," he said. The thickness in his voice sent a tremor rumbling through her, stirring a reaction she thought had died with his departure.

He stepped forward, filling the door frame until they were inches apart. The tremor gained intensity, until it felt like a storm was building within her, churning in her belly. He reached down and hooked his forefinger under her chin, lifting her face to his.

She waited, breathless, to see what he would do. Behind him, the holiday lights on her neighbors' homes sparkled in the background like a million multicolored stars, giving the world—this moment—an unreal, almost magical feel. She knew it should be cold, felt the wind blowing past and around them, saw their breaths mixing and rising into the air. All she registered was heat, from that small spot where his finger met her chin, the only place where they were touching, from his eyes poring over her face and staring deep into her own.

Then, as though granting her something she'd been waiting an eternity for, he finally lowered his mouth to hers.

KERRY CONNOR

SILENT NIGHT STAKEOUT

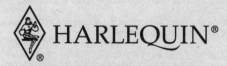

HARLEQUIN®

TORONTO • NEW YORK • LONDON
AMSTERDAM • PARIS • SYDNEY • HAMBURG
STOCKHOLM • ATHENS • TOKYO • MILAN • MADRID
PRAGUE • WARSAW • BUDAPEST • AUCKLAND

Many thanks to Allison Lyons
for her enthusiasm for this story.

With gratitude to all the Harlequin Intrigue authors
whose books made me dream of joining their ranks,
for showing me how it's done.

ISBN-13: 978-0-373-74557-9

SILENT NIGHT STAKEOUT

Copyright © 2010 by Kerry Connor

Recycling programs
for this product may
not exist in your area.

ABOUT THE AUTHOR

A lifelong mystery reader, Kerry Connor first discovered romantic suspense by reading Harlequin Intrigue books and is thrilled to be writing for the line. Kerry lives and writes in New York.

Books by Kerry Connor

HARLEQUIN INTRIGUE
1067—STRANGERS IN THE NIGHT
1094—BEAUTIFUL STRANGER
1129—A STRANGER'S BABY
1170—TRUSTING A STRANGER
1207—STRANGER IN A SMALL TOWN
1236—SILENT NIGHT STAKEOUT

CAST OF CHARACTERS

Regina Garrett—A client's murder turns the defense attorney into a target herself.

Marcus Waters—The homicide detective has an instinctive dislike for defense attorneys, but isn't about to let that stop him from solving this case—and keeping Regina safe.

Jeremy Decker—He knew something someone would kill to keep quiet.

Lauren Decker—If Jeremy's sister knows what secrets her brother was keeping, she isn't telling.

Jeff Polinsky—Marcus's partner doesn't bother to hide his dislike of Regina.

Cole Madison—Is the wealthy man a simple crime victim, or something more?

Tracy Madison—A woman who is possessive toward what she considers hers.

Donald Gaines—A man with powerful connections and no qualms about using them.

Eric Howard—How much does Jeremy's childhood friend know?

Troy Lewis—Lauren's ex-boyfriend is nothing but trouble.

Adrian Moore—His responsibilities extend far beyond his job description.

Prologue

Jeremy Decker sat in the driver's seat of the parked car, hands clenched on the steering wheel, and tried to fight the fear gripping his body.

The feeling was nothing new. It seemed as if he'd spent the past year being afraid, ever since the night the police had arrested him. He still remembered the shock and terror of those moments when they'd slapped the cuffs on and dragged him away. The first days after the arrest had been nerve-racking because he hadn't known what would happen next. Then there'd been all the long months in jail when he'd been scared to sleep, scared to turn his back on anyone, scared that he'd never see the outside again.

But never in his life had he been as scared as he was right now.

Outside, the temperature was almost zero. A thick layer of snow was on the ground, the wind blowing gusts of it across the deserted street. He knew the cold had to be seeping into the vehicle more and more every moment he sat there. White puffs of air appeared in front of his face with every breath he took. He barely felt it, unable to feel anything but the fear holding him in place.

He didn't make a move to restart the engine and turn on the heat. It would only delay what he needed to do. He needed to push the door open. He needed to get out of the car and walk into the office building where his lawyer was waiting for him. He needed to get help.

He needed to tell.

Just the thought of it made him swallow hard, his lungs tightening painfully in his chest. The idea was terrifying, no matter how much he knew he had to do it. Ms. Garrett would know what to do. She'd fought hard for him, done everything she could for him, gotten him out of jail.

Now, though, he couldn't help but wish she hadn't fought so hard, had left him there, where it suddenly seemed so much safer.

Lost in his thoughts, he barely had time to react to the sound of the back door being wrenched open before someone slid into the seat behind him.

He jerked his head up to meet the intruder's

eyes in the rearview mirror. He felt no surprise at what he saw. There was only the fear, rising another notch to outright horror.

"Does she know? Did you tell her?"

He somehow managed to make his throat move, to force out the sound. "No."

"But you were going to, weren't you?"

There was no point in lying. He was sure the answer was written all across his face. He couldn't keep it from his eyes as they stared back at those in the mirror.

Staring at those eyes, he never saw the knife. He only felt it, the pain sharp and swift and agonizing against his neck. His mouth fell open in shock, in terror. He couldn't move, couldn't find the power to utter a single word.

He could only stare into those eyes as they stared back, grim and determined.

Before he realized it, he felt it, the cold, in a way he hadn't before. It poured into his body, insistent and unrelenting, filling him down to the bone. Until he could feel nothing else.

Cold. So cold.

And then he felt nothing at all.

Chapter One

"Tell me you're not still at the office."

Bracing the phone between her ear and shoulder, Regina Garrett smiled at the dismay in her friend's voice. "I answered the phone here, didn't I?"

"You're supposed to be on vacation!"

"And I will be, just as soon as I see one last client." A client who was already more than an hour late, she noted with another glance at the clock. Jeremy Decker had practically begged her to see him, so if anything, she would have expected him to be early. But an hour after their designated meeting time, he had yet to appear. She wasn't sure whether to be concerned or annoyed, though annoyance was starting to win out.

"There's always one more client with you," Cheryl said. "That's the reason you haven't had a vacation in three years."

Four, Regina thought, not about to correct

Cheryl when she was already in mid-lecture. The last thing her friend needed was more reason to get riled up.

"Not this year. This really is the last client. My calendar is cleared for the next three weeks, my bags are packed and tomorrow morning I'll be on a plane."

"Uh-huh. I'll believe it when I see it."

"I booked the flight and the hotel long ago, and both are nonrefundable. I'm going."

"I guess that's something. You might be a workaholic, but I've never known you to throw away money like that." Sounding slightly mollified, Cheryl sighed. "Christmas in the Caribbean. I really envy you."

"You wouldn't miss Christmas with your family for anything," Regina pointed out.

"I know, but I wouldn't mind exchanging all this snow and ice for a sunny beach. The tropics will sure be a big change from Chicago."

"You've got that right. It'll be nice to get some actual sun in December." It would be even nicer to have the kind of Christmas Cheryl had in store for her, with her kids and husband and multitude of assorted relatives, all squeezed together in a house that wasn't really made to accommodate so many people. But they would make do, and be happy, laughing and eating and loving, just enjoying being together.

Regina swallowed the pang of envy as she pictured it. Ever since her mother's death, she'd been alone for the holidays. There was no other family left, and unlike Cheryl and pretty much every one of her friends, she was still single. Meeting the right man wasn't easy in her line of work. As a criminal defense attorney with her own small practice, she worked long hours, and bad guys were more likely to cross her path than good ones. And given how she spent her days, it was even more important to her that any man she spend her nights with be a good one, someone real and honorable and true. Sadly, such men seemed to be a rare breed, or if not, all the ones out there were already taken.

She knew Cheryl would have invited her to spend Christmas with her family. She had a dozen other friends who would have done the same if she hadn't told them her plans. Though her friends would have gone out of their way to make her feel nothing but welcome, she still would have felt like an intruder, the pathetic interloper piggybacking on somebody else's Christmas, somebody else's family.

But not this year. This Christmas she was going to sit on a beach and do her best to forget about work and the holidays, with nothing on her schedule but enjoying the sun and having hot island men serve her drinks with little umbrellas in them. If that was the closest she was going to get to meeting a good man this year, then so be it.

But first she needed to deal with her one last, incredibly late client, she thought with another check of the clock.

On the phone, Cheryl continued to prattle on about Regina's island getaway and her own holiday plans, with nothing more than Regina's automatic murmurs of agreement in response. That was Cheryl, perfectly capable of having a conversation with herself.

Finally Regina had to interject, "You know, I think my client's finally here. I should go."

"Yes, you should," Cheryl said sternly. "You know I'll call back in a little while to make sure you're gone."

"I won't be here."

"Good. If I really don't talk to you again, you be sure and call me the minute you get back. I want to hear all the details."

"I promise," Regina said with a smile. "Merry Christmas, Cher."

"Merry Christmas!"

With a wistful sigh, Regina replaced the phone. Around her, the empty office was heavy with silence and shadows, the lights in the outer room already shut off to conserve power. She'd sent her assistant home to her own family hours ago. It was well after seven o'clock and she suspected there was no one left in the entire building.

Not for the first time, she wondered why Jeremy could possibly need to see her so badly. She'd tried to get him to tell her on the phone, but he'd only said that he needed to talk to her about something important. She'd done her best to tell him it would have to wait until the new year, but he'd been so insistent she'd finally relented and named the meeting time that had passed well over an hour ago.

As far as she knew, his case was closed. He'd been arrested early in the year for burglary after being found in the middle of the night outside a home on the North Side. A friend in the public defender's office had called her about the case, knowing she had the time and resources to serve him better than they could and that it was the type of pro bono case she was likely to take. Jeremy Decker was a young man with an otherwise spotless record who'd needed help. And she'd done her best to help him, working long months to have the charges dropped and him released in time to spend Christmas with his sister, who'd just given birth a few months ago to a niece Jeremy had never seen.

He'd been released only a few days ago. She couldn't imagine he'd managed to get in any new trouble since then, and his old trouble had already been resolved.

Reaching for the phone, she called the number for the house Jeremy shared with his sister. Again, there was no answer, not even a machine or voice mail. If he had a cell phone, she didn't have the number.

When the clock hit two hours past the agreed-upon meeting time, Regina finally decided she'd waited long enough. Whatever Jeremy wanted, it couldn't have been as urgent as he'd said if he couldn't make their meeting or call with an explanation. She'd given him enough of her time. Besides, she didn't know what more she could do for him. As far as she was concerned, her work on his case was done.

She quickly moved through the office, making sure everything was shut down and closed up tight, then retrieved her briefcase and headed for the door. Minutes later she was pulling out of the parking garage beneath the building, her mind already turning to the last few tasks she had to accomplish before her flight in the morning. As soon as her tires hit the slush on the street, her anticipation for those tropical beaches kicked up another level. It really would be nice to get away.

She was only a few yards from the building when her headlights swept over a familiar car parked on the opposite side of the street in front of her. She automatically eased off the accelerator, all thoughts of her vacation evaporating. It was Jeremy's car, or at least a dead ringer for the one she knew he owned. Apparently he was here after all. Had she just missed him on her way out of the building?

She slowed to a crawl as she neared the vehicle. The street was dark, night having fallen hours ago, but there was enough light from the nearest streetlamp that she could make out a figure sitting in the driver's seat.

She waited for him to roll down the window or acknowledge her in any way.

Nothing happened.

Pulling over to the curb, she climbed out of the car and checked both ways before crossing the street to Jeremy's vehicle. There was still no motion inside. She leaned down toward the window, already raising her closed hand to tap on the glass.

The first thing she saw was the blood. There was so much of it that half the front seat seemed to be smeared with redness. Most of it was centered on the figure sitting there. Her eyes slowly trailed upward from the blood coating the person's chest, past the awful gash on his throat, already knowing what she'd find before she saw his face.

Jeremy Decker stared straight ahead, the emptiness in his eyes showing he was dead even if she hadn't seen all that blood. His mouth gaped as open as his throat, and shoved between his lips was what appeared to be a red handkerchief.

Reeling back in horror, Regina struggled to pull in a breath. Over the years she'd seen the grisliest of crime scene photos, but not once had she ever seen a murdered body in the flesh. To have the victim be somebody she knew made it even worse.

Jeremy. She'd seen him just days ago. Happy and excited, and most important, alive, eager to meet his niece.

Regina hurried back to her car for her cell phone, trying to choke back the sadness and regret that threatened to overwhelm her. Just moments ago, she'd been annoyed with him for being late, sitting in the safety of her office while someone did this to him right outside.

It appeared Jeremy Decker had the best excuse for lateness there was.

Chapter Two

"I'll never understand people," Jeff Polinsky griped as the crime scene came into view in front of the car. "You'd think cold like this would keep them indoors instead of running around outside killing each other."

"I guess it depends how badly they want to kill somebody," Marcus Waters mused from the driver's seat. "You know as well as I do some people aren't going to let anything stop them."

"Yeah, just like I know if there's an outdoor crime scene in December, we're the ones who are going to catch it."

With a faint grin, Marcus simply shook his head at Polinsky's complaining. He'd heard this particular refrain before. They'd been partners for almost two years, and Marcus would be hard-pressed to think of a single day Polinsky hadn't found something to complain about. A big, burly and balding figure in his fifties, Polinsky had been on the job for a long time, and the man wasn't exactly known for his charm. Marcus knew that the reason they were partners wasn't just because they worked well together, but because he was one of the few who were able to tolerate the man. For all Polinsky lacked in personality, he was a good detective, and that was all Marcus cared about. He just let everything else roll off him.

Not that he could disagree with Polinsky on this one. A nighttime crime scene in temperatures flirting with zero wasn't his idea of a fun evening, either. Even with the heater blasting, the inside of the car was barely warm. He could imagine how it would feel when they got outside in the open.

But they would do it, and they would deal with the cold. Somewhere in the mess of people and vehicles in front of them was a victim, and somewhere out there was a killer. And it was their job to find that person and make sure he or she didn't get away with it.

Familiar determination spread in his gut. He'd been on the job long enough he probably shouldn't still get the feeling. Not nearly as long as Polinsky, but long enough that the idea of a new case, a new perp to catch, shouldn't still give him a charge. But after all these years, the feeling was still there, still as strong as ever.

He found a free spot along the curb that was as close as they were going to get and parked the car. Before he'd even put the vehicle in Park, Polinsky had shoved his door open and begun the laborious process of hefting his frame out of the car. Marcus met him in front of the sedan and they started toward the scene.

A multitude of flashing lights lit up what he figured would normally be a quiet street at this time of night. It was a business district, primarily office buildings and a few warehouses, the kind of area that would be mostly deserted by now. A uniformed officer broke away from the scene and came to meet them as they approached.

"What do we have?" Marcus asked when they were face to face.

"Male victim found in his car. He's been identified as Jeremy Decker, age 24."

"Who identified him?"

"His lawyer. Regina Garrett. She's the one who found the body. Her office is just up the street."

Marcus frowned at the same time Polinsky echoed, "Regina Garrett?"

"Yeah. You know her?"

"I've heard of her," Polinsky muttered, his tone making it clear none of what he'd heard had been good.

Marcus wasn't surprised. He'd heard of Regina Garrett, too, all from other cops, none of whom had been fans. She was a defense attorney, and a very good one at that. Word had it she was smart, she was tough, and she was a crusader. If there was a weakness in a case or the slightest angle to be exploited, she'd find it. More than one case had been torpedoed over the years thanks to her. He'd never dealt with her on one of his cases or encountered her personally, but he'd heard enough to know he wouldn't like her.

He did his best to swallow the instinctive distaste. Logically speaking, he knew defense attorneys served a key role in the justice system. But he also knew that in all likelihood there were plenty of people who should be in jail but weren't because of her.

"If she's the vic's lawyer, I'm assuming he's had some trouble with the law," Marcus said.

"Burglary," the officer confirmed. "She got him out a few days ago, just in time for Christmas."

Polinsky snorted. "I bet he's wishing she hadn't right about now."

"She's waiting over there if you want to talk to her."

"In a minute," Marcus said without bothering to see where the officer gestured. He knew talking to her was necessary, but was in no hurry to do so. He could already guess how much fun dealing with her was going to be. Regina Garrett could wait. "Let's take a look at what we've got first."

"Sure, but I've got to warn you, it isn't pretty."

"They usually aren't," Polinsky grumbled.

It took only one look to see the officer hadn't overstated things. Marcus had certainly seen his share of crime scenes over the years, but this one packed an unpleasant punch that was uniquely its own. Even Polinsky winced and glanced away for a second, muttering under his breath, before refocusing on the body.

Jeremy Decker stared straight ahead, expression frozen in a look of terror. He'd known he was going to die, probably felt it happening as all the blood that coated his front poured out of his body. He'd had his throat cut from behind, presumably by someone seated in the back seat. The back driver's-side door was unlocked, most likely from the killer's exit and possible entrance if he or she hadn't been inside the car all along, but there weren't any useful footprints that could be discerned outside the vehicle. They'd have to hope there was some useable trace evidence within the car, but from the looks of it, it hadn't been cleaned in some time, making it unlikely anything would be found.

With one last look, Marcus turned to Polinsky. "Guess we should talk to the lawyer. You want to take her?"

"Nah, you go ahead. I might say something I regret."

Knowing Polinsky, that was a safe bet. Nodding tightly, Marcus suppressed a sigh and turned around, eyes seeking out the woman, already anticipating what he'd find. No doubt she'd be uptight and humorless, a know-it-all with her nose in the air ready to tell him how to do his job and make it as difficult as possible. She'd probably be irritated at having been forced to wait instead of being spoken to immediately. He looked for someone who was frowning, someone who looked ready for a fight—

Someone who was drop-dead beautiful.

He stopped and almost did a double take as soon as he saw her. And there was no doubt this was her. The cold had limited the number of onlookers. There were relatively few women around, and all the rest were part of the crime scene team. That left a single female standing alone on the fringes.

Despite the cold, she wasn't hunched over in her coat trying to keep warm. She stood straight, hands in her pockets, her eyes on the scene, as though she wasn't affected by the weather at all, even as the wind pulled at the edges of her coat. A streetlamp behind her poured its glow directly over her, illuminating her as effectively as a spotlight. Which, from the looks of her, was exactly where this woman deserved to be.

Even from a distance, there was no mistaking the beauty of that face, her features perfectly formed, her lips lush and full, her skin a dark, warm brown. Her coat was belted at the waist and molded to her body, hinting temptingly at lush curves. Despite her obvious beauty, she didn't look as cold and unapproachable as such women often did. Certainly not the angry, arrogant figure he'd been expecting. There was a warmth, a kindness, to her face, something approachable despite the worry on it that made her infinitely more appealing.

Their eyes met across the distance. Hers widened slightly with surprise, with shock, with something he recognized all too well as a charge suddenly jolted through his body. He stood as frozen as the world around him, but all he felt inside was raw heat.

Now that he thought of it, he'd heard talk that she was a looker, but mostly in a "what a waste" sense, her appearance hugely over-shadowed by the talk of everything she'd done. What she did.

He would be better off remembering that. Not that he had any trouble doing so. After all, the only reason they were both here, the only reason he'd had the opportunity to ex-perience that sudden, inexplicable charge that had passed between them, was because she'd gotten another criminal freed.

The only thing that mattered was finding out if her actions had played as much of a part in getting him killed.

REGINA HAD SEEN THE man she deduced was a homicide detective as soon as he ar-rived with another man who appeared to be his partner. He'd been far enough away, with his collar pulled up against the cold, that she hadn't been able to get a good look at him. She'd watched from a distance as he and the other man had approached Jeremy's car and examined the gruesome scene she could still see entirely too well in her head.

But it wasn't until he suddenly turned and looked directly at her that she was able to see him clearly. And in that instant when their eyes met, every thought that had been racing through her head evaporated, along with every bit of moisture in her mouth.

The man was, quite simply, the best thing she'd seen in a long time, so much so he almost didn't seem real. He was tall, with the kind of muscular frame that not even the bulky coat could hide. It seemed barely capable of containing his wide shoulders, the sleeves stretching and straining around his arms. Even if she hadn't been able to see the rest of his body, his face would have been enough to tell her what it was like. His features were all hard planes and sharp leanness, and even his cheekbones seemed to have muscles. His hair was cut close to the scalp, making the features on that dark brown face stand out that much more strongly.

He started toward her, that massive frame moving with an easy grace. Her heart did a curious lurch in her chest, then kickstarted again in a faster pace as she watched his approach.

Then he came close enough that she could see the tightening of his expression, the wariness in his eyes. She immediately knew the cause of his reaction, and she choked back a sigh.

So he was one of those. A cop who viewed her as the enemy.

She wasn't surprised, of course. It went with the territory. She was comfortable with her career. She'd learned a long time ago that the police weren't always right and that not all police officers were good people. But there was still something uniquely disappointing about having as fine a male specimen as the man before her looking at her like that.

She swallowed the disappointment that rose in her throat. Hadn't she just been thinking how difficult it was to find a good man? She should know better than to let herself be so affected by a physical reaction, a reaction that was no doubt caused just as much by the stress of everything that had happened in the past few hours as the man himself. Finding Jeremy. Talking to the first officers on the scene. The endless waiting. It was no wonder her emotions were off-kilter. She sucked in a breath, trying to regain her senses.

Then he was in front of her, bigger and more overwhelming than before, and she suddenly had to try to recover from his appearance all over again. "Ms. Garrett?"

Damn. His voice was as sexy as the rest

of him, a low rumble she felt quake through her. She nearly shuddered. "Yes," she said, her tone admirably smooth.

"Detective Marcus Waters," he said, all business. "I was told you found the body."

The subject matter thankfully brought her back down to earth. "That's right."

"And the victim was a client of yours?"

"Yes. He called earlier this evening and asked to see me."

"About what?"

"He didn't say. I tried to get him to tell me, but he would only say it was very important. I was expecting him at six. I called him a few times when he didn't show, and finally gave up around eight. I was driving by when I saw him."

"And he was already dead?"

"Yes."

"You represented him on a burglary charge, is that correct?"

"That's right."

"Did he do it?"

For a second, the blunt, wholly unexpected question caught her off-guard, as she suspected he'd intended. Fortunately she had plenty of practice at keeping her expression from re-vealing anything but what she wanted it to. She never blinked, meeting his gaze head-on.

"The charges were dismissed, Detective. That makes him innocent in the eyes of the law."

"That's not what I asked."

"I'm afraid anything he might have told me is covered by attorney-client privilege."

"Even if it's relevant to his death?'

"Even then."

The corners of his mouth twitched, turning downward the slightest bit, the only sign of his displeasure. She had to fight the urge to stare at those dangerously tempting lips. "What *can* you tell me about the case?"

"I imagine not much more than you could find in the police file."

"Since I don't have the file on me, any insight you could provide would be appreciated," he said with a trace of sarcasm.

"Jeremy was arrested in April after the police responded to an alarm indicating a break-in at a home in Lincoln Park. He was found at the scene and was unable to provide a reasonable explanation for his presence, so he was arrested and later charged with burglary."

"You said the charges were dismissed. So the case never went to trial?"

"No, it never got that far. He was released a few days ago."

"And was murdered soon afterward."

"You think there's a connection."

"Wouldn't you?" he said sensibly. "Or maybe I should ask, don't you?"

"I can see why you would think that," she said carefully.

"So is there anything you *want* to tell me about the case? Anything I should know?"

Regina sighed. "Detective, I promise I'm not trying to be difficult. I want whoever did this to Jeremy to be caught just as much as you do. But frankly, it's been a rather difficult evening and I'm not at my best. Let me take a look at my notes when my head's a little clearer and see what I might be able to share with you."

Eyes narrowed, he looked at her, long and probing, his gaze feeling as though it was peeling away the layers of her skin and exposing her to the core. Finally, his expression eased, like he'd come to the conclusion she really wasn't trying to be a pain. "I would appreciate it."

"Has his sister been informed?"

"His sister?"

"Lauren. She's his next of kin, the only family he had left other than the baby she had a few months ago."

He nodded. "I'll take care of that next."

"I'd like to be there when you do."

"Why?"

"Lauren Decker just lost her only sibling. She's going to need a kind face to break the news."

"This isn't the first time I've had to inform someone of the death of a family member."

"A family member you didn't view as nothing more than a no-good criminal? That's what you've already decided, isn't it? That Jeremy Decker was nothing but a lowlife who probably deserved what was coming to him?"

"I'm not sure anyone deserved this, but just because you got him off doesn't mean he was truly innocent."

"And just because he was arrested doesn't mean he was guilty."

From his expression, he was biting back the response he wanted to offer. After a moment, he said, "Either way, I'm capable of breaking this news to her gently."

"Then I look forward to seeing that. Because Lauren Decker is a young woman who just had a baby, which she is raising on her own. I suspect her emotional state is already fragile, and I can't imagine this news is going to help that. Besides, who do you think she's more likely to confide in, someone she just met who's a member of the same police department that recently arrested her brother, or someone she's met before, someone her brother trusted?"

Regina could tell he wanted to argue the point, those lips now compressed into a thin, frustrated line.

"Besides, like you said, you don't have the file, so you'd have to look up the address. I already know it."

"Fine," he practically growled. "You can come."

"Thank you." Inwardly, she sighed with relief. Evidently she'd been wrong earlier. She could do something else for Jeremy Decker, the same thing she'd always intended to do: make sure he got justice. And not even an incredibly handsome police detective was going to prevent her from doing so.

The sound of footsteps crunching on slush and snow indicated someone was approaching moments before the man she'd seen arrive with Waters came up behind him. He was middle-aged and overweight, the folds of his face seemingly settled in a permanent frown. Even so, she had the distinct impression his scowl was extra fierce for her benefit, given the bleary-eyed glare he shot at her. Another cop who didn't like her, she registered, though the knowledge gave her none of the disappointment she'd experienced when she'd seen the look in Detective Waters's eyes.

"Everything okay over here?" the new-comer asked.

"Fine," Waters said. "Ms. Garrett, my partner, Jeff Polinsky. Polinsky, Regina Garrett. Ms. Garrett has graciously agreed to provide the address of the next of kin. We're going to go notify her now."

The man's frown deepened. "*She's* going? Why?"

"To help," Waters said with a wry edge that hinted at his skepticism. "You coming?"

"Pass," Polinsky muttered, the look he shot her leaving little doubt for the reason. "I'll wrap things up here, get a ride back with somebody."

"Fine."

Both men turned back toward her at the same moment. Regina knew Polinsky was about to challenge her before he said a single word. "Since you have all the answers, how about it, Counselor? Any theories about why somebody killed your client?"

Regina didn't flinch from his stare, refusing to let his hostility get to her. "I have to assume someone didn't want him to talk about something."

"Oh, yeah? What makes you say that?"

"Why else shove a red handkerchief or whatever that was in his mouth? It was a message."

"Probably. Especially since that handkerchief most likely didn't start out red."

"Polinsky—" Waters started.

She frowned. "What are you talking about?"

"The handkerchief was red from the blood." The corner of his mouth curved in a smirk, the nasty pleasure in it instantly making her uneasy. "The killer cut out his tongue."

Chapter Three

"I apologize for Polinsky," Marcus said as he drove them toward the address Regina Garrett had given him. "He's not usually so rude."

"Somehow I doubt that," she said mildly from the passenger seat.

His mouth twitched in acknowledgment. "I'm not saying he's not rude. He's just not usually *that* rude."

"I understand. He's not the first cop who didn't like me, and I doubt he'll be the last."

"That doesn't bother you?"

"Like most people, I'm not crazy about the idea that anyone dislikes me. But then, I wouldn't be very good at my job if the entire Chicago PD were fans."

"Well, cops tend to not be too crazy about people who help criminals get off," he said before he could think better of it. As soon as the words were out, he braced himself for an angry comeback.

Instead she simply said, "Everybody deserves a defense, Detective. It's how our justice system works."

He didn't bother to disagree. He was well aware how the justice system worked, or at least how it was supposed to. He also knew that some people deserved nothing but to be punished. That was justice. He almost asked her how many who deserved to be punished hadn't been because of her, how many crimes they'd gone on to commit, how many people they'd hurt because she'd given them the opportunity. But that would make him no better than Polinsky, and he was in no mood to pick a fight.

They passed the rest of the trip in silence, his discomfort growing by the minute. He did his best not to look at her. It didn't help. He could still see her out of the corner of his eye, still feel her presence with almost painful awareness. The faint scent of her perfume, something light and distinctly feminine, seemed to fill the close confines of the car, and every bit of his senses.

He felt a spurt of relief when they finally reached the street she'd named. It was nearly eleven o'clock. Most of the houses on this quiet residential block were aglow with holiday lights, though their darkened windows indicated that almost all of the residents were settled in for the night. He slowed as the house numbers began to reach the one he sought.

"I think that's it," she said a second after he spotted the house. It was a small one-story structure with a single car parked out front. Unlike those around it, this house wasn't decorated with any lights. There also didn't appear to be any on inside, at least none that were visible from the front.

"Was it just Decker and the sister who lived here?"

"I believe so. From what I remember, they inherited the house from their father, who died a few years ago. Their mother died when they were children."

Filing the information away for future reference, he parked along the curb in front of the house and climbed out. He might have opened her door for her, but by the time he rounded the vehicle she was already out of the car. She started for the house as soon as he joined her, moving so automatically he almost wondered if she'd waited for him or intended to go on her own and leave him to follow.

Before he could bring up how they would handle this, she strode right up to the front door and knocked. For more than a minute, there was no answer.

"She may already be in bed," Marcus observed.

"Maybe," Regina agreed. "Especially if she managed to get the baby to sleep. She'd probably be trying to get as much rest as she could. I hate to wake her." She sighed. "I hate to tell her any of this."

To his surprise, there was genuine regret in her voice. She meant it. Frankly, he'd taken her insistence on being here as evidence of the control-freak tendencies he'd initially assumed she'd have, her claims of concern nothing more than a ploy to have her way. She was a lawyer; of course she'd be good at making an argument. Her obvious sincerity caught him off-guard, nearly made him look at her again until he managed to catch himself.

She was about to knock again when the curtains in the window shifted slightly, then the sound of locks being withdrawn met their ears. The door finally, slowly eased open. A nervous-looking face, a female version of Jeremy Decker's, peered at them over a still-fastened chain. "Yes?"

"Hi, Lauren. Do you remember me?" Regina asked.

After a moment, Lauren nodded shakily. "You're Jeremy's lawyer."

"That's right. This is Detective Waters

with the Chicago Police Department. Can we come in? We need to talk to you about something."

"Jeremy's not here."

"I know. We need to talk to you."

Lauren's expression said she wanted to say no. Finally, as though realizing how futile it would be to turn away the police, she grimaced. "I just got the baby to sleep. You'll have to be quiet."

"Of course."

The door closed long enough for her to unfasten the chain before opening it fully. She was dressed in threadbare sweats, her hair wet as though she'd just stepped out of the shower. They hadn't woken her, apparently catching her on her way to bed instead. As Regina had said, she was young, looking to be barely in her early twenties. Even younger than her brother. She was pretty, but tired-looking, probably to be expected for a woman with a baby. She waved them in, quickly closing and relocking the door behind them, then turned to face them, folding her arms almost protectively over her chest.

"Is there somewhere we can sit down?" Regina asked when it looked as if Lauren Decker wasn't going to offer.

Lauren nodded tightly and stepped past

them to lead the way into a tiny living room off the entryway. She motioned vaguely at the couch, as much as an invitation as it seemed like they were going to get, falling into a chair herself.

Regina slid onto the edge of the couch closest to Lauren. Marcus remained standing, not seeing any way he could fit on it with her, not really wanting to get that close.

"Lauren, I'm afraid I have some sad news," Regina said slowly, the kindness in her voice again catching him by surprise. "Jeremy is dead. I found him in his car outside my office tonight. He was murdered."

He watched Lauren's reaction to the news. She blinked several times, a lack of comprehension in her expression. It was a face he'd seen more than once in moments like this. "What are you talking about?" she said, her voice barely more than a whisper.

"It appears someone killed him while he was sitting in his car."

Eyes wide, Lauren began to shake her head. "Who?"

"That's what we were hoping to ask you," Marcus said gently, ignoring the look Regina shot him. "Do you have any idea why anyone would want to hurt your brother?"

She blinked up at him, her gaze slowly

sliding from his to Regina's, then away entirely as she lowered her head. And he knew before she said a word that she was going to lie.

"No."

Before he could call her on it, Regina leaned forward. "Lauren, I know you must want whoever hurt Jeremy to be held responsible. If there's anything you can tell us, anything at all, it would be helpful."

This time the pause was barely noticeable before Lauren shook her head. "I'm sorry. I don't know. He'd only been home a few days, and we didn't talk much. He didn't want to talk about jail, and he went out a lot."

"Do you know where he went or who he went to see?" Marcus asked.

"No. Like I said, we didn't talk much."

He was about to press her further when Regina interjected. "Okay. I know this is a lot to take in, and we should give you some time to grieve."

Before she even finished speaking, she started to rise. Marcus's first instinct was to object. He hadn't even begun to ask the many questions he had for Lauren Decker. But if he tried to press on in the face of Regina Garrett's kindness, he would just come off like a bully, and that wouldn't get him anywhere. As he took in the face of the young woman before him, now even more drained and pale than when they arrived, it was clear she'd closed herself off to them. He might be able to get more out of her now, or maybe he'd do even better once she'd had a chance to let the news and the implications of her brother's death sink in.

Regina reached out and touched the arm of the young woman, who'd also risen. "Are you going to be all right here alone, or is there someone we can call to be with you?"

Lauren shook her head. "We don't have any family left, and I have the baby. She'll probably wake up if I have anyone over. I'll be okay."

Regina reached into her purse and pulled out a business card. "Here's my number. Please call me if you need anything."

"Thank you."

Marcus already had his own card in hand. "And if you think of anything you think might be helpful, feel free to call me."

She took the card without meeting his eyes. He didn't believe for a second she would use it, but wanted to keep his name in her memory. Because like it or not, they would be meeting again.

Lauren Decker knew something, and sooner

or later—sooner if he had any say in the matter—he was going to find out what it was.

"SHE WAS LYING," Detective Waters said as he pulled away from the house.

"I know," Regina said without hesitation. She should have known he'd pick up on it as well as she had. There was something reassuring about that. It implied he was smart, good at his job. He might be the right man to solve Jeremy's murder after all.

"I would have appreciated the chance to talk to her further rather than have you rush us out of there."

"It was obvious she wasn't going to tell us anything. I have a feeling you saw that as well as I did."

"It couldn't have hurt to try."

"Couldn't it? She was a clearly exhausted woman who barely had time to absorb her brother's murder. If you pushed her too far she could have turned against us entirely and decided to never cooperate at all."

"Me," he corrected. "She could have turned against me. There is no 'us.'"

No, there certainly wasn't, she thought with a pang. The comment seemed best left unaddressed. "Either way, you're better off giving her a chance to let this sink in. Once she has a chance to think about it she may decide to share what she knows. If not, then you can push her. Or does your partner usually play the bad cop? I have a feeling he's good at it."

"He is," he admitted. "In the meantime, is there anything *you* want to tell me?"

"What do you mean?"

"You know, if you were right and the killer was sending a message, that message was most likely intended for you."

He wasn't telling her anything she hadn't already considered, but hearing him voice the possibility made it much harder to ignore. She swallowed the knot that rose in her throat. "I know," she agreed.

"It would seem somebody wanted to prevent him from talking about something. If there's even the slightest chance he told it to you, they might come after you."

"As I reminded you, attorney-client privilege applies to anything Jeremy might have told me."

"We're talking about someone willing to slit your client's throat and cut out his tongue in a car parked on the street. I have a feeling this isn't someone who's going to take a chance you'll remain that dedicated to your principles."

"Which means this also isn't someone likely to take the chance I don't know anything either," Regina said on a sigh. "And believe it or not, I really don't think I know anything anyone would be willing to kill to keep hidden. I have to believe Jeremy was going to tell me tonight and didn't get the chance." If only he had. If only she'd pressed him harder on the phone. He might not be dead, or if so, at least she might have some idea what she was facing.

"Of course this is all guesswork," he said after a moment. "For all we know whatever warning the killer implied wasn't intended for you."

He was trying to make her feel better, she realized with surprise. She glanced at him, and for a moment, their eyes met. At the sight of that impossibly good-looking face, a nervous flutter erupted in her chest. She tried to read his expression for any hint of what he was thinking, but came away empty. It was an odd reassurance for him to offer her. She wouldn't have thought he would bother. She wondered what it meant that he had, wondered if it meant anything at all.

Wondered why she cared. No point reading too much into a simple courtesy.

"I hope you're right," she said, unable to keep the doubt from her voice.

They'd reached the street where her office was located. It hardly seemed possible but the crowd of police officers and crime scene technicians was already gone, the street deserted. As they neared the space where Jeremy's car had been parked, the place where he died, she saw there was nothing there now. The body had been removed, the car towed away. But the memory of what had been there remained vivid in her mind, and she couldn't suppress a shudder.

He stopped next to her car and put his vehicle in Park. As she unbuckled her seat belt, he reached into his coat and pulled out a business card, offering it to her. "For when you've gone over your notes, or if you think of anything else."

"Of course." Tucking the card in her pocket, she opened the door. "Good night, Detective."

"Take care of yourself, counselor," he said in that low, smooth voice of his, what should have been no more than a basic parting line sounding strangely personal.

She crossed the street to her car, fully expecting him to drive away as soon as she was out of the vehicle. He didn't, remaining where he was as she unlocked her car and started the engine. Only when she was heading down the street did she see him finally start to drive away, his lights fading from view in her rearview mirror.

The fact that he'd finally left made sense. The fact that he'd waited until she was safely on her way, while somewhat surprising, was understandable.

The fact that she felt better for his having done so, or that the warmth caused by the timbre of his voice and those closing words continued to linger long after he was gone, was much harder to explain.

WHEN HER ALARM WENT OFF the next morning, Regina was jolted out of an uneasy sleep that was anything but restful. Instantly wide awake, she stared at the glowing digits on her bedside clock. It was early. She'd forgotten to reset the alarm the night before. This was the time she'd needed to get up to catch her flight to the Caribbean.

A flight she wouldn't be taking, she acknowledged without a second thought. Shutting off the alarm, she rose to her feet and padded to the bathroom. All that mattered was finding out who was responsible for what had happened to Jeremy Decker.

Going to bed hadn't allowed her to escape the horror of last night's events. Her dreams had been filled with images of Jeremy, first silently begging her for help he was voiceless to explain, then as he'd looked when she'd found him, long past asking for anything.

And almost just as disturbing, an unsmiling police detective with dark eyes that seemed to sear through her, his expression mysterious and unreadable no matter how long she tried to discern what he was thinking.

Regina didn't let herself linger on the last image. There were much more important things to deal with. She needed to get to the office and go through Jeremy's file. With any luck, there would be something in it that would help her figure out this mess.

She showered and dressed as quickly as possible, already deciding to stop for coffee on the way rather than take the time to make it. Within fifteen minutes she was ready to go. Making her way downstairs, she tugged on her coat and, ignoring the packed suitcases lined up by it, pulled the door open.

She was about to step outside, her gaze lowering as she fumbled through her keys, when she saw it.

There was something on her front porch.

She froze, her keys forgotten. The snow

hadn't reached the porch, so the object, stark white against the brown of the wood, was plainly visible—and immediately noticeable as out of place. She stared at it for a moment, unsure what to do. Peering closer, she tried to identify it. It was white. Some kind of paper? No, the texture was wrong. It looked like some kind of fabric. Almost like—

A handkerchief.

Dread held her in place for a moment, her mind automatically going back to the last handkerchief she'd seen, the one shoved in Jeremy Decker's gaping mouth. The one she'd thought was red.

The handkerchief most likely didn't start out red.

No, in order to end up that color of red, it must have started out white. As white as the handkerchief sitting on her front porch.

And it was just sitting there, slightly crumpled or folded over. It didn't move other than the edges fluttering the slightest bit. A cold wind was blowing outside. She could feel it swirling around her ankles. Yet the handkerchief didn't blow away. Something must be holding it in place.

And in a horrifying instant, she knew what it was.

Her mind immediately rebelled, her stomach

nearly doing the same. The idea was too terrible to consider. She desperately tried to think of another explanation, and came up blank.

Still, she had to know.

Digging into her bag for a pen, she inched closer to the handkerchief. Coming only as near as necessary, she leaned in, using the pen to ease back the corner of the fabric where it was folded over.

One glance was all it took to see her instincts had been correct.

Expecting it didn't protect her from the shock of seeing it herself. She reeled back, already wishing she hadn't looked, already trying to block out the image.

If the killer was sending a message, that message was most likely intended for you.

Detective Waters's words echoed faintly from the back of her mind.

Waters.

She should call him. She should call somebody. It only made sense that it should be him. Even as the thought occurred to her, she was reaching into her pocket for the business card he'd given her, then for her cell phone.

She forced herself to focus on the tiny digits on the card and dialed the number with trembling fingers.

It took only two rings for him to answer.

"Waters."

The sound of that voice sent a rush of relief through her, the emotion fiercer than she had any business feeling.

"Detective Waters, this is Regina Garrett."

There was the briefest of pauses before he responded. "Of course, Ms. Garrett. What can I do for you?"

"I'm at home. There was something on my front porch when I opened my door this morning."

"What kind of something?"

"A white handkerchief. And there's something in it. I think—" She swallowed hard, tried to force the words out when her throat just wanted to gag.

"I think I found Jeremy Decker's tongue."

Chapter Four

If there had been any question whether the removal of Jeremy Decker's tongue was supposed to be a message, Marcus figured its arrival on Regina Garrett's porch provided a pretty definitive answer. From the look on her face, she knew it as well as he did.

It was a message, all right—a message that now had literally been delivered to her.

Not that he spent much time looking at her face. He deliberately avoided it, keeping his eyes on his notebook as he took her statement about what had happened.

Unfortunately, for more reasons than one, there wasn't much she could tell him and he soon ran out of questions. "I guess that does it," he concluded, finally looking up with some reluctance. "Unless there's anything else you can think of that might be helpful?"

"There isn't," she said firmly. "I didn't see or hear anything."

He wasn't surprised. The tongue hadn't been there when she'd arrived home, so it must have been delivered in the middle of the night while she was sleeping. Polinsky was checking with the neighbors to see if anyone had seen the person who'd left it. Marcus doubted anyone had. Even if one of her neighbors had been awake at that hour, he suspected the perpetrator would have done everything to make it impossible for anybody to identify him or her. It shouldn't have been a difficult task, given the weather and the kind of bulky winter clothing most people were wearing these days. This person seemed determined to prevent Regina from revealing something. After going to this much trouble, they weren't going to risk having their identity revealed by getting caught leaving the tongue on her porch.

He also didn't doubt the tongue had been left by the person who'd cut it out of Jeremy Decker's mouth in the first place. It wasn't exactly a gift someone could ask a second party to deliver. It was too personal. Everything about this was too personal.

Marcus didn't tell Regina Garrett any of that. She looked unsettled enough—rather understandably, he thought as he studied her. They stood in her living room—she'd declined the opportunity to sit—as the crime scene techs photographed what she'd found on her porch and collected it for evidence. Her expression was calm, but her posture gave her away. She was ramrod straight, her spine stiff, her arms folded over her chest. One hand stroked up and down the opposite forearm absently as though she was subconsciously trying to comfort herself. His gaze lingered on the motion, and he felt something clutch in his chest.

"Are you sure you're okay?" he asked before he could stop himself.

"I'm fine," she said with a tight smile, then sighed gently. "At least as fine as I can be. I'm past the initial shock of finding…it at any rate."

He nodded, not sure if he should believe her.

As though confirming his doubts about her emotional state, she cleared her throat softly and asked, "Is it all right if I use the bathroom?"

"Of course."

With a tight nod she turned and started out of the room. When Marcus realized he was watching her walk away, he immediately lowered his eyes and slowly exhaled, releasing the air that had been pent up in his lungs.

He'd spent the past twelve hours trying not to think about Regina Garrett. Her open, lovely face. Her soft, inviting scent that had stayed in his vehicle long after they'd parted ways. It should have been easy. God knew he had plenty of other things to think about, a million other subjects fighting for his attention. But somehow his thoughts had kept being pulled back to her. Even after he'd gone to bed, he'd lain awake for far too long, and what he'd thought about was her.

Then, just when he'd finally settled in at work that morning and found the means to push her out of his mind, she'd called with the news of her discovery. And so here he was, in the home of a woman he couldn't seem to get out of his head. A woman who, despite the shock of what she'd found, looked even better than he'd remembered.

He gave his head a brief shake. He didn't know what it was about her that had grabbed his attention so firmly and refused to let go. Yes, she was beautiful, but he'd met beautiful women before. Maybe not as beautiful, maybe not in the same way, but beautiful nonetheless. Yet there was something different about this woman. From the very first moment he'd seen her, he'd responded to her in a way he never had to any woman before and couldn't seem to shake. But whatever the reason, this wasn't the time and these really weren't the circumstances for him to be thinking about her like that. He was pretty sure he had no business thinking about this particular woman at all.

Seeking a distraction, Marcus scanned the interior of her home, trying to get a sense of the woman who lived here—strictly for the case. It was a two-story, single-family house, and she'd already told him she lived alone. It wasn't the kind of place he would have pictured her living, but the woman seemed to be full of surprises, and now that he was here, he had to admit it seemed to fit her.

She appeared to be neat, but not fanatically so. There were enough signs that the room was lived in—a few magazines tossed on the coffee table, an afghan loosely folded at the end of the couch—without too much unnecessary clutter. There were no Christmas decorations on display. She had no tree, no wreath on the door. Even in the light of day, he'd noticed that hers appeared to be the only house on the block without any lights or displays outside. It was something they had in common, he acknowledged before he could think better of it. He hadn't bothered with any decorations at his place, either.

Not comfortable with the comparison, Marcus glanced toward the front door, hearing the sounds of Polinsky talking to the techs outside. He noticed, not for the first time, that there were two matching suitcases lined up neatly in the entryway, as though ready and waiting to be carried out.

He was staring at those bags when she reentered the room. She did look better now, like she'd taken the opportunity to gather herself. If anything she looked even more beautiful.

He saw she'd noticed where his attention had been focused. He made himself ask the logical question. "Going somewhere?"

"I'm supposed to be on vacation at the moment," she explained. "I had a flight out this morning, but obviously I couldn't go."

That explained the lack of holiday decorations both inside and outside her home. She hadn't expected to be here for the holidays. He wondered where she'd been going, who she'd been going with. A boyfriend? He pushed the thought aside. Whatever the answer, it was none of his business.

Polinsky chose that moment to walk through the door. "The guys are done out here. They're going to take off. What about you?"

"Yeah, I think we're done," Marcus said. "You get anything from the neighbors?"

"Nobody saw anything." Polinsky turned his attention to Regina, the gleam that entered his eye sending a warning through Marcus's system. "Pretty nasty Christmas present, huh, counselor? Must have given you quite a scare."

On the final words, his mouth twitched. Marcus had to fight back a sudden surge of anger. When she'd called to report her discovery, Polinsky hadn't been able to keep from smirking, seeming to take a particular pleasure at the news. Not unexpected given how he felt about her, but not one of his finer moments as far as Marcus was concerned. It was one reason he'd insisted on taking Regina Garrett's statement, even though he hadn't really wanted to and Polinsky had been more than willing to talk to her in this instance.

Regina met Polinsky's gaze calmly, seeming unruffled by his hostility. "It was certainly an experience I could have done without."

"So how about it, counselor? Seems pretty clear somebody doesn't want you talking about something your client told you. You ready to tell us what that is?"

"As I've already told Detective Waters, I don't know what it is."

"I know what you told him. I thought this might have jogged your memory."

"My memory is just fine, and I can't be reminded of something I never knew."

From the way his lip curled, Polinsky didn't believe her. Marcus wasn't surprised. Considering Polinsky's feelings and everything he'd heard about her, it made sense he would assume she was trying to be difficult, keeping relevant information from them, viewing him as much the enemy as he did her. The only truly surprising part was that Marcus didn't feel the same way. He believed her. He just wasn't sure he wanted to examine his reasons for that belief.

Before he could say anything, Regina turned toward him. "I've been thinking. We need to talk to Lauren Decker again. Now that she's had a chance to absorb the news of Jeremy's death, she may be more forthcoming."

Marcus didn't miss the glance Polinsky shot him at her comment, and knew exactly what had caused the reaction. "There is no 'we,' remember?" he told her. "I let you come along last night to break the news to her, but that's taken care of."

"Fine, I'll rephrase. *I* need to talk to Lauren Decker, and I was offering to let *you* come as a courtesy. Because I *am* going to talk to her, and while we could speak with her separately, we've both seen which of us she responded to more. Chances are, the only way you're going to learn anything is if you're with me when I speak with her."

He wanted nothing more than to argue with her logic. He needed her out of this, for multiple reasons. Trouble was, she was right. Lauren Decker had appeared to respond better to Regina than to him, certainly more than she would to Polinsky. His partner's bulldog tactics might actually get something out of her, but Marcus wasn't sure he felt right about siccing the man on her, especially when she just lost her brother less than twenty-four hours earlier. And if Regina did manage to get something out of the young woman, he didn't want to learn about it secondhand, if she bothered telling him at all.

"All right," he said, barely managing to keep it from sounding begrudging. "'We' will talk to her one more time."

"Great." She nodded, her expression much less smug than he might have expected since she'd gotten her way again.

"Waters, can I see you outside?" Polinsky asked.

Marcus grimaced. If he couldn't already guess this wouldn't be pretty, the dangerous tone in Polinsky's voice made it clear. "Sure," he said, swallowing a sigh. "I'll be right back," he told Regina.

She nodded, sending an uneasy glance between him and Polinsky, as though sensing the undercurrents between them. He would have been surprised if she hadn't.

Polinsky had already pushed through the front door. Marcus followed, stopping when Polinsky whirled to face him at the bottom of the front steps.

"What the hell are you doing?" Polinsky demanded in a hushed tone.

"What's best for the investigation."

"The woman is lying. She knows a hell of a lot more than she's admitting. Letting her be involved in any part of the investigation is a mistake. For all we know she's just trying to get in the way to obstruct it, the same way she is by not talking."

"I don't believe that. We both saw her face when we first got here. She knows what that tongue meant and she got the message loud and clear. She knows her best bet is for this person to be caught."

"Or she got the message and decided to take it to heart and make sure whatever they don't want told doesn't come out."

"No way," Marcus said without hesitation. "I'm the one who spent time talking to her last night, remember? She wants her client's killer caught. You really think that woman in there, the one we've both heard plenty about, is going to cave because someone threatens her? Does that sound like the Regina Garrett you've heard about?"

Polinsky's silence told Marcus he'd scored the point.

"Besides," he continued. "She's right. She can be an asset we can use. This is about solving the case."

"Really? It's not about you wanting to spend more time with her?"

"Of course not." It was true. He really didn't want to spend any more time with her.

So why did it feel like a lie?

Clearly that was exactly what Polinsky thought it was. He shook his head. "Right. Do what you want. I'll see you back at the station."

"You're not coming again?"

"*I'm* not interested in spending any more time with Miss Bleeding Heart in there."

Polinsky started to turn away, only to stop and glance back. "Watch yourself, Waters. She may be nice to look at, but don't forget who she really is and what's underneath the pretty face."

With that parting line, he stomped away,

leaving Marcus to stare after him and ponder his words.

Though Polinsky wouldn't have believed it, he really didn't need the warning. He knew he had to watch himself around this woman. The way she'd dogged his thoughts, that strange protectiveness he felt around her, made that clear enough. Most important, though, was the fact that she was involved in the case, and as always, that was all that mattered: the case. Anything that could interfere with that had to be avoided. That included distractions as sizeable as Regina Garrett, regardless of who she was and what she did—both of which were reasons enough in their own right.

He knew it, just as he already knew the resolution was going to be hard to live up to. In fact, the only thing he didn't know was why.

Or maybe, he thought, his heart sinking into his gut, he just didn't want to know, since the answer threatened to be even more disturbing than what Regina Garrett had found on her front step that morning.

"I GOT THE FILE ON THE burglary your client was charged with," Detective Waters said as he drove them back to Lauren Decker's house.

"That must have made for some interesting reading," Regina said mildly, though inwardly she started gathering her energy for the upcoming debate. She knew everything he must have read, of course, and she was pretty sure she knew what conclusions he must have drawn. Which meant she was going to have to defend her client again, this time to him.

She was prepared to do it, and Lord knew she'd never been one to back down from an argument. The trouble was, she was having a harder than usual time focusing.

Because of him.

They were back in the close confines of his car, the small space accentuating his sheer size, his presence a palpable thing she couldn't begin to ignore even when she wasn't looking at him. He was too big, and she felt him too keenly, her skin practically buzzing with awareness of his closeness.

He was even better looking than in her dreams. She'd opened the door and been struck by it, the same way she'd been the first time she'd seen him, her heart simultaneously leaping into her throat and kicking into a higher gear. More than that, she'd been glad to see him again, an excitement that went far beyond simple relief that he'd come to help her with what she'd found. The feeling had remained as he'd taken her statement, until she'd had to excuse herself to get away from it—and him—for a few precious moments. Even now, her heart continued to beat faster than normal.

She wasn't used to this feeling, wasn't entirely sure she liked it, was positive she wasn't comfortable with it. What was it about this man that caused such a reaction within her? Yes, he was good-looking, but this was something more than that, something entirely too disturbing. She was an intelligent woman. She believed in logic and reason. And there was nothing logical or reasonable about the level of response she had to this man.

"You have to admit, they had plenty of reason to charge him," Waters said finally, dragging her attention back to the subject at hand.

"Possibly," she said, unwilling to concede even that much. "They certainly didn't have enough for a conviction."

"I wouldn't be so sure about that. Look at the facts. The first officers responded to a silent alarm at the home of Cole and Tracy Madison. When they arrived, they spotted your client fleeing the scene. He didn't live in the neighborhood and couldn't explain his presence, and his fingerprints were later found on the back door window the burglars broke to get in. I don't know about you, but I've seen people convicted on less."

"That doesn't mean it was enough to convict in this case. Clearly, the ASA agreed, since she decided to drop the charges."

"Just because the State's Attorney's office decided the case wasn't a sure enough thing to make it worth their time to pursue doesn't mean they couldn't have gotten a conviction."

"I doubt it, not with all the unexplained questions. There were plenty of grounds for reasonable doubt. For starters, the Madisons reported several items stolen in the burglary, mostly jewelry belonging to Mrs. Madison. Jeremy wasn't found in possession of any of those items."

"It was considered likely that the burglary was committed by more than one person. His accomplice could have gotten away with those pieces."

"Except there's no proof there was more than one burglar. Then there's the matter of the fingerprints. Anyone over the age of ten knows about fingerprints, and any would-be criminal would do everything they could to keep from leaving any. Jeremy didn't even have gloves in his pockets when he was arrested, and there were none discarded nearby. Jeremy wasn't stupid, nor was he intoxicated or in any way impaired when they found him. Yet we're supposed to believe he tried to commit a burglary and was foolish enough to leave his fingerprints on the broken window? It doesn't make sense."

"People aren't always smart, especially criminals. They make mistakes. Why else would his fingerprints be there?"

"Maybe he was passing through the alley behind the house, saw the broken window and decided to investigate. He could have touched the glass by accident."

He exhaled sharply. "You really think that story makes more sense than the official theory?"

"I'm just saying it's another possible theory. You can't prove it's not true any more than you can prove yours is. That's what reasonable doubt is all about."

"Be honest with me. After everything that's happened in the past twenty-four hours, you really still think he was innocent?"

"I think it's not safe to assume he wasn't. We don't know that the murder was connected to his arrest."

"Really? Because as far as we know, Jeremy Decker's arrest and his murder have one thing in common: you. *You* represented him, *you* found him outside your building, and *you* found his tongue on your front porch. It seems pretty clear somebody doesn't want you talking about something they thought he told you. What else would someone think he told you about but the burglary?"

"I don't know," Regina said. "Believe me, I wish I did."

"I would guess that there was an accomplice, the person who got away with Mrs. Madison's jewelry. Most likely that person wanted to silence Decker to keep him from revealing his or her involvement."

"Except Jeremy had gone all those months without implicating anyone else, and now the charges against him had been dropped. Why would he have turned on that person now, and risked renewing suspicion in his own involvement?"

"Maybe they had a falling-out. That person would have had the goods all this time, maybe even sold them by now. It could be they didn't want to share once Decker was out of jail. Decker came to you for advice—maybe he was being threatened. The accomplice silenced him and now wants to ensure you don't reveal him or her."

It made more sense than Regina wanted to

admit, except for one thing. "For any of this to be true, Jeremy would have to be guilty, and I still don't believe that."

"If he wasn't involved, then why was he there? Why was he even in that neighborhood?"

"I can't say."

"I respect your loyalty to your client, counselor, but at this point, wouldn't it be more loyal to help find out who's responsible for his death?"

"That's what I'm doing."

"Then tell me what he told you, what explanation he offered for being there."

Regina sighed. "I can't do that."

Silence hung in the vehicle. She felt Waters look at her, practically felt her skin tingle under his scrutiny. She kept her eyes focused on the street in front of them, not wanting to give him the chance to read anything in her expression.

"No," he said finally. "You really can't, can you? I'm guessing he never gave you an explanation, did he? Did he even tell you he was innocent?"

She didn't say anything, still not wanting to admit it, even though she suspected her continued silence was answer enough.

As expected, Waters made a noise of

disbelief. "If Decker didn't tell you he was innocent, then why are you so determined to believe he was?"

"Because I talked to him. Because I looked him in the eye and got to know him. In my line of work, I often have nothing to depend on but my instincts. I suspect the same is true in yours."

She glanced at him. He didn't respond. As had been the case with her, she suspected that signaled an agreement he'd never admit.

"Besides, if you're right, why wouldn't he have lied and just told me he didn't do it?" she continued. "Why say nothing at all? My gut told me it was because there was more to the story. Jeremy Decker had never gotten into a hint of trouble in his life, he had a decent job, and yet he suddenly decided to start committing burglaries? It didn't make sense."

"From the looks of his car and his house, not to mention the fact that he couldn't afford to make bail and had to stay in jail all those months, he couldn't have had a lot of money. Plus, his sister was pregnant and you told me she's raising the baby on her own, so the father must not be in the picture. Decker could have needed money fast and gone looking for an easy score."

"I don't believe things were desperate

enough that he'd just decide to do something like that out of nowhere."

"People change, Ms. Garrett. Every person who ever broke the law had a first time. Just because they hadn't done it before then didn't mean they were never going to."

"True. But most people who've never broken the law never will. Whatever the explanation, the case was weak and Jeremy needed my help. I was determined to give it to him."

"Why didn't you just admit that you don't really know whether or not he was guilty?"

"I wanted you to keep an open mind. I didn't want you to jump to any conclusions that might color your opinion of him and adversely affect your handling of the case. I'm guessing that now that you've decided that he didn't even tell his own attorney he was innocent, you've probably decided he must be guilty after all."

"Like you said, I have to depend on my instincts."

"Understood. And in this case, my instincts are telling me the situation is more complicated than a simple burglary. I think Jeremy's death proves that."

He didn't disagree with her. He didn't respond at all. She finally glanced at him to find him peering through the windshield, his eyes narrowed. She realized with a start they'd reached Lauren's neighborhood without her noticing and had just pulled onto Lauren's street.

Regina's eyes immediately went to the house. Lauren was standing on the front step talking to a man. Something about the man's posture, the way he was leaning in, towering over the young woman, instantly put Regina's senses on alert, even from down the block.

"Waters—" she started.

"I see them," he said grimly, his tone as on edge as her own.

As they drew nearer, Regina could see Lauren's arms were wrapped around herself, her posture defensive. The door was shut behind her, and it looked as though the man practically had her backed up against it.

Waters pulled up to the curb in front of the house, right behind a luxury sedan that was already parked there. The car had barely stopped moving before Regina launched herself from it.

The man glanced back, no doubt having noticed their arrival. Regina only got a brief impression of a hard face bearing a cold expression before he returned his focus to Lauren, murmuring something low that Regina couldn't make out as she approached.

From the way Lauren's eyes remained pinned on his face, her chin tightening, her cheeks darkening, she hadn't missed a word.

Regina was halfway up the front path to them when the man spun around and headed in her direction. He didn't even glance at her as he slid past on his way to the street. He didn't need to. Regina kept her gaze on him, memorizing every inch of his face. He was in his late-thirties, muscular and blunt-featured, with dark brown eyes and black hair. His mouth had a cruel twist to it, his thin lips compressed. He was wearing a long coat, and Regina caught a glimpse of a suit beneath it. She was tempted to stop him, to ask what had been going on here. She didn't believe for a second the man would bother answering.

As soon as he'd passed her, Regina turned her attention to Lauren. The young woman stared past her, eyes fixed on the departing man. Taking in her expression, Regina had to reassess her earlier opinion. It wasn't fear radiating from Lauren Decker's face and every line of her body. It was anger.

Regina came up to her. "Lauren, are you okay?"

"I'm fine," Lauren said in a monotone, still looking past her.

"Who was that man? Was he threatening you?"

Lauren shook her head. "No. He's nobody. It's not important."

Unconvinced, Regina glanced behind her. The man had climbed into his car. Its engine started, and a few seconds later, the vehicle began to pull away from the curb.

The sound of a car door slamming shut drew her attention to Waters's vehicle, which he had only just exited. She wondered what had taken him so long. He gave no indication as he strode up the path to her and Lauren, his attention focused on the younger woman.

"Lauren, is everything okay?" he asked when he reached them.

Lauren swallowed, lowering her eyes. "Sure," she said tightly.

Regina didn't believe her for a moment. Rather than press the point, Waters said, "In that case, could we go inside? We'd like to speak with you if that's all right."

Lauren looked like she wanted to say no, but she finally just sighed, her shoulders slumping. "Fine." She turned and was about to open the door when she stopped, her hand on the knob, and glanced back at them. "Just keep quiet. I put the baby down for a nap."

At their nods, she pushed the door open

and let them in. They once again moved into the living room. This time Lauren didn't sit, simply faced them, her arms folded over her chest. "What is it?"

Still disturbed by what she'd seen and hoping for an explanation, Regina was about to say something when Waters stepped forward first.

"Lauren, Ms. Garrett and I both saw that man confronting you outside. After what happened to your brother, I can't help but be concerned. Is someone threatening you? Because if you're in some kind of trouble, I can help you, but I have to know what it is. All you have to do is tell me and I'll do whatever I can."

Regina looked at him in surprise. From another man the words might have come across as manipulative or intimidating, as though he was trying to take advantage of what they'd observed to get her to open up to him. There was none of that in his statement. Regina believed him. There was no denying the warm sincerity in his voice, the firm promise in every word, the honest, straightforward way he met Lauren's eyes. He meant it. If Lauren was in trouble, he would do everything he could to help her.

A wholly unexpected warmth filled Regina's

chest. This was a side of him she'd never seen before. With her, even when he'd asked her if she was all right back at her house, there'd always been a cool reserve about him, like he was holding her at arm's length. The man before her now exuded compassion, as though he were ready to draw Lauren in and shield her from harm. Whatever he thought of her brother, he was willing to help the young woman.

Lauren evidently wasn't as moved as she was. Her expression didn't change. "It was nothing," she said flatly.

He studied her for a long moment, but rather than press her further, he simply nodded, his face betraying no disappointment or disbelief. "All right. We do need to ask you a few more questions about Jeremy."

"I don't know what I can tell you."

"Yesterday your brother contacted Ms. Garrett saying it was urgent that he meet with her. Do you have any idea what he wanted to meet with her about?"

"No." Frowning, Lauren looked at Regina. "Don't you?"

"I'm afraid not," Regina said. "He didn't say on the phone and he was killed before we were able to meet."

"Did Jeremy ever talk to you about his

arrest and the burglary he was accused of being involved in?" Waters asked.

Lauren shook her head. "Not really. He didn't want me to come to see him in jail. I don't think he wanted me to see him like that. And after he came home, I think he just wanted to forget about the whole thing."

"Do you believe he did it?"

"No," she said. "Jeremy wouldn't do something like that."

"You do know his fingerprints were found on the glass of the window that was broken to get into the house."

"That's what the cops said."

"And you never asked him how that could be?"

"No."

"Do you have any idea why he would have been in that neighborhood at that time of night?"

Lauren shrugged a shoulder. "No."

If Waters felt the slightest impatience at her lack of answers, he didn't show it. He simply nodded, his expression solemn, revealing nothing. He glanced away, his eyes briefly traveling over the room before returning to the young woman.

"You said Jeremy went out a lot since he came home. Can you give me the names of some of his friends, some of the people he might have gone to see?"

"I don't know...."

It was such a simple question Regina had to tamp down her own irritation at how the young woman was stonewalling him. She was tempted to jump in, but Waters's expression remained steady and patient. He simply walked over to a nearby bookcase and lifted a framed photograph Regina hadn't even noticed from the shelf. Moving back to Lauren, he held the photograph out to her. "What about the man in the picture with him? They look close. What's his name?"

Regina glanced at the image in the frame. It was a graduation photo. Jeremy and another young man roughly the same age as him stood dressed in their caps and gowns, their arms slung around each other, big grins on their faces as they faced the camera. Waters was right. Clearly the men were friends, especially if the photo was deemed worthy of framing and keeping on display.

"That's Eric Howard," Lauren said after a long moment. "They grew up together."

"Based on the presence of this photo, I'm assuming they may have kept in touch and are still close."

Lauren pressed her lips together, then nodded. "Yes."

"Do you know where he lives?"

"Not really."

Again, Waters didn't appear bothered by the vague answer. "That's all right. I can find out. I appreciate your help." Regina was impressed by the lack of irony in his tone. "I think that's all I need at this time. If you think of anything you believe I should know, please give me a call. Do you still have my number?"

Her brow furrowed, as though confused by the fact that he wasn't pressing further, Lauren nodded again.

He turned and headed back to the door. Lauren moved forward as though to usher them out, leaving Regina no choice but to follow him.

At the exit, Waters opened the door and stepped out. Rather than do the same, Regina stopped and turned back.

"I know it's still early and you may not have even had a chance to begin thinking about funeral arrangements or anything else. Do you have anyone to help you with that?"

From the way Lauren frowned, Regina suspected the young woman hadn't even considered it. "I'll figure it out."

"Well, if you do need help with absolutely

anything, please let me know. I truly cared about Jeremy, and I promise we're going to do everything we can to figure out who's responsible for what happened to him."

"Thank you," Lauren said faintly. If she took any comfort in the words, she didn't show it. She looked pale and tired, almost unbearably young in the oversize sweatshirt she wore. It hardly seemed possible that she could remain on her feet, let alone deal with everything she must be facing. Regina wished there was something she could say to get the young woman to confide in her, but she suspected there was little chance of that happening at this point.

Trying to set aside her misgivings, Regina nodded and stepped through the doorway. Almost immediately, she heard the door close behind her.

Waters was standing on the sidewalk by his vehicle, his cell phone at his ear. As she approached, he apparently ended the call and lowered the phone.

"Everything all right?" she asked.

"I ran the plate on the car of the man Lauren was talking to when we arrived. It's a company vehicle registered to Gaines Financial Services."

Regina immediately made the connection.

"The company where Cole Madison works and where Tracy Madison's father is the president and CEO."

"Was that Madison?"

"No. I've seen a picture and that wasn't him."

"Well, if it wasn't Madison, then it must have been someone from his company."

"But why would someone from his company come to the house of the man accused of robbing him?"

"There's only one way to find out."

"What's that?"

He arched a brow, a spark of amusement in his dark eyes. "We ask Madison."

She didn't miss the fact that this time it was he who'd said "we." She matched his raised brow. "You're not going to argue over me coming along?"

"Would it do me any good?"

"Not at all."

"I didn't think so. At least this time you're admitting I'm letting you come along."

"*This* time," she agreed.

The tightening of his mouth indicated he wasn't ready to grant her the point. "Well, I wouldn't put it past you to try to talk to the man on your own. It's better for me to be there to keep you from causing too much trouble and hurting the investigation."

The implication stung slightly. Rather than let it show, she let a slow smile lift the corners of her lips. "Good to know you think so highly of me. Whatever the reason, I appreciate it, Detective Waters."

He looked at her for a long moment, his steady focus sending an unexpected heat to her face. "Marcus," he said roughly. "It's Marcus."

Nothing he could have said would have surprised her more. It was just his first name, nothing more than a courtesy he was extending her. But somehow it seemed like more than that, more intimate, as though a barrier keeping some distance between them had been removed. Given how off-kilter she already felt in his presence, she wasn't sure that was a good thing. Yet, in spite of herself, she felt a sudden, ridiculous pleasure at the gesture.

"All right," she said slowly. "Marcus, then. And it's Regina."

Lowering his eyes, he nodded sharply without commenting, then turned to round the front of the car.

Once his back was to her, Regina took a breath before opening the door on her side, needing to collect herself for a moment before climbing into the small space with him. His reaction told her all she needed to know, what she already should. He saw her as the enemy. Whatever the reason for the gesture, she shouldn't read anything into it. He didn't like her, didn't respect what she did, and she had no interest in being with a man who felt that way about her career or who she was.

At least that's what her head said.

Too bad her body didn't seem to be listening.

Chapter Five

"What exactly do you know about Cole and Tracy Madison?" Marcus asked as they headed uptown. It was the main reason he'd allowed her to come. As he'd told Polinsky, she was a resource. At this point, he had to believe she knew more about the parties involved in the case than he did.

"They've been married for seven years," Regina said. "Though it may be eight by now. Cole Madison is in his late-thirties, his wife roughly five years younger. No children. Tracy Madison's father, Donald Gaines, is the president and CEO of Gaines Financial Services, an investment firm. Cole is some kind of VP. He worked at the company several years before marrying the boss's daughter."

"Do you know of any connection between the Madisons and your client other than the burglary charges?"

"No. I had my investigator do a background

check to see if she could find anything, but nothing came up. Although I didn't have her check for connections between Jeremy and every single person at the company, just the Madisons and their immediate family and the company in general, and even that was just to be safe. Maybe I should have gone deeper. Maybe we missed something."

Her words had taken on a troubled tone. He glanced over to find the same emotion in her expression. She seemed truly bothered by the idea. He could almost see her wondering whether this possible oversight had led to Decker's death.

"Gaines Financial has to have at least several hundred employees," he pointed out. "It wouldn't have been reasonable to try to connect Decker to every single one of them. Besides, was there any reason to suspect a connection between Decker and the company at all?"

"No," she admitted.

"Then it sounds like you went above and beyond anyway. Your job was to get him off and you did that."

"'Get him off' implies he was guilty," she said pointedly. "My job was to defend him."

"And you did it," he said, figuring it wasn't worth arguing the distinction. "How did you manage to get them to drop the charges anyway?"

"It really wasn't that difficult. The case was paper-thin and I just kept going back to the ASA assigned to the case with all the holes and unanswered questions until she was forced to admit it. Frankly, given the weaknesses in the case, I was surprised it took as long as it did. I sort of suspected she was under some pressure to continue the case for some reason."

"Pressure from whom?"

"Her boss. Maybe the Madisons, or, more likely, Donald Gaines. The Madisons are wealthy, but Gaines is much more so, and I suspect he has the connections to push the case through if he'd wanted to. If there was pressure being placed by someone, that person must have changed his or her mind, because the State's Attorney's office finally decided to drop the charges." She sighed. "At the time, I thought that was a good thing. I really wanted Jeremy to be released by Christmas. I guess he would have been better off if I hadn't."

Marcus frowned. "You don't really believe it's your fault."

"No. The only person to blame is the person who killed him. It's just hard not to think about how different things might have played out if

I hadn't done my job quite as well. Or maybe done it better and gotten him to confide in me sooner. The reason I didn't push harder was because I didn't think it was necessary to defend him. The case was weak enough I didn't need anything more to get it dropped. If it had proceeded to trial, I would have worked harder to get him to tell me more. But since it didn't, I didn't. I guess I should have."

She lapsed into silence. He glanced at her again. Clearly it was what she was thinking about, and judging from her expression, what she would think about for some time.

Troubled himself, he tried to focus on the road. He'd wondered what effect her actions might have had on Jeremy Decker's death, had almost assumed there'd been one. He just hadn't expected her to be bothered by the idea. He wanted to believe she was that kind of defense attorney, the kind with no scruples who'd do whatever it took to get her sleazeball clients off. But she clearly cared about Jeremy Decker, was obviously bothered about what her own role might have been in his death, and that bothered *him*. It meant she had a conscience, a sense of morality, and it would be a lot easier—for him, at least—if she didn't.

Uncomfortable with his thoughts, he cleared

his throat. "For all we know there was no connection between Decker and the Madisons before the robbery. That man, whoever he was, might have been there *because* of the robbery."

He saw her look at him. "For what reason?"

"Just because your client was released doesn't mean everybody was convinced he was innocent. Tracy Madison's jewelry is still missing. The Madisons could think their best hope of getting it back is to talk to Decker."

"Then why threaten Lauren, if that's what was happening?"

"They or their man might not know Decker's dead. Lauren could have either refused to tell him, or if she did, he might have decided to try finding out what she knew."

Regina nodded slowly. "It's possible. Maybe we'll find out when we talk to Madison."

Yes, Marcus thought, and hopefully they'd learn something useful, something to get him closer to solving this case. The more time he spent with this woman, the more it seemed that couldn't come soon enough.

THE MAIN OFFICES OF Gaines Financial Services were located in a high-rise downtown just off the Loop. Parking in the garage under the building, they took the elevator up to the thirty-fifth floor.

The young woman stationed at the reception desk looked up as they exited the elevator and approached her. "Good afternoon. Welcome to Gaines Financial Services. May I help you?"

Marcus pulled out his badge. "Detective Marcus Waters. I'd like to speak with Cole Madison."

The woman's eyes widened slightly, though her pleasant expression never changed. If she was curious why he hadn't introduced Regina, she didn't show it. She simply reached for the phone on her desk with a polite, "One moment."

Regina glanced at Marcus, wondering exactly how he intended to deal with her presence. They hadn't discussed it in the car, and she couldn't exactly ask him at the moment.

After speaking in hushed tones into the receiver, the receptionist finally hung up and turned her attention back to them.

"Mr. Madison will be right with you."

They stepped aside out of the way. A minute later, a man emerged from the hall to the right of the receptionist's station. Regina identified him immediately as Cole Madison. He stopped to speak with the receptionist, who pointed him toward Marcus.

"I'm Cole Madison," he said, striding toward them. "I believe you were asking for me?"

He was a fit, handsome man who could easily pass for several years younger than the late-thirties Regina knew him to be. She had no doubt he was fully aware of that fact as he greeted them with a smile, flashing flawless teeth, his voice and posture projecting an easy confidence. If he was at all nervous to be summoned by the police, he didn't show it, his expression displaying nothing but idle curiosity. Because he had nothing to hide, or because he was good at hiding his true feelings?

"Detective Marcus Waters. This is…my associate, Regina Garrett."

If Cole Madison noticed that slight hesitation before Marcus explained who she was, he didn't outwardly react. He nodded politely toward her before returning his attention to Marcus. "What can I do for you, Detective?"

"Is there somewhere private we could speak?"

Madison hesitated, as if he wanted an answer to his question first. Then he sent a glance around the reception area and seemed to think better of continuing the conversation here. "Of course. We can use my office. It's right this way."

He turned and led them down the corridor he'd emerged from until they arrived at a corner office. It was exactly what she would have expected for a man in his position. The scenic view through the windows on two sides and the elegant yet understated wood furniture combined to give a sense of status and stability, as though the office's occupant would be the perfect person to entrust with one's money.

He didn't offer them seats, nor did he take his behind the desk. He remained standing, facing them.

"Now then, if you could tell me what this is about…"

"I'd like to speak with you about Jeremy Decker," Marcus said.

The man didn't so much as blink. When Marcus didn't elaborate, Madison frowned, shaking his head slightly. "I'm not familiar with anyone by that name."

"He's the young man who was arrested for the break-in at your home earlier this year."

Madison nodded. "Oh, of course. I thought

that matter had been settled. I was notified the charges were dropped."

"Did that bother you?"

"Not really. So much time has passed and the insurance already covered the losses. At this point, I've pretty much moved on from the incident. I still don't understand what brings you here. Are you still investigating the break-in?"

"No, we're investigating Jeremy Decker's murder. He was killed last night."

The man's eyes widened in surprise. It was the expected reaction to that kind of news. Regina just couldn't tell if the response was genuine or faked.

"My god," Madison said. "Do you think what happened is connected to the break-in?"

"We're pursuing all possibilities," Marcus said blandly.

"Well, I'm not sure how I can help. My wife and I weren't home when the robbery occurred, and we never met this Jeremy Decker."

"Earlier this morning, a man paid a visit to Jeremy Decker's sister. The vehicle he was driving was a corporate car registered to your company. You wouldn't happen to know anything about that, would you?"

Regina watched Cole Madison's reaction closely. Again, there was none, but there was something a bit too studious about his lack of response, something that made it seem less than genuine. "Not at all."

"So you're saying the visit wasn't made at your request?"

"No. Of course not. Why would it?"

"It just seems strange that someone from your company would pay a visit to the Deckers. I'd very much like to speak to the man who was driving the car. Do you know how many vehicles are registered to your company?"

"I have no idea."

"Well, I have the license plate number. Is there any way you can find out who had the car this morning?"

"I suppose I could look into it, have someone pull the records to see who was assigned that car."

"That would be very helpful, thank you."

Marcus pulled out a business card. Consulting his cell phone, he wrote down the number on the back of the card and handed it to Madison.

The man had barely taken it when the door behind them suddenly opened. "Cole, are you ready—"

Regina turned to see a woman had entered,

recognizing her as Tracy Madison. A slim brunette in her early thirties, she was stylishly dressed, her clothes and accessories expensive yet tasteful. Regina recognized it as the carefully constructed look of a woman who had so much money she knew it would be tacky to flaunt it too much, and enough vanity to make sure people knew it just the same. Though she was attractive, there was a hardness to her face that wasn't, taking away from the overall effect. Her hair and makeup were flawless, and she was wearing a long winter coat, hat and gloves, indicating she had just arrived or was on her way out.

Eyebrows lifting, she swung her gaze between Marcus and Regina. "I'm sorry. I didn't realize you were in a meeting," she said, and though Regina couldn't have said why, she didn't believe her.

An older man, his features close enough to the woman's to make it clear they were related, had entered behind her. Like the woman, everything about him spoke of money, not just the cut of his suit, but the casual arrogance of his expression. His face was even harder than the woman's, his features sharp and severe, his chin slightly lifted so that it seemed as though he was looking down at everything. As he took in the scene, his eyes narrowed, his gaze flicking over Marcus and Regina before centering on Madison and narrowing further.

"Not a problem," Madison said. "This is Marcus Waters and Regina Garrett with the Chicago Police Department. Detectives, allow me to introduce my wife Tracy and my father-in-law, Donald Gaines."

"Is something wrong?" Gaines asked.

"It seems the young man who was accused of breaking into our house was murdered last night," Madison said quickly.

Tracy Madison's eyes widened a fraction. "That's terrible. Do you think it's connected to what happened at our house?"

"We're still investigating at this point," Marcus said.

"But you believe that's the case," Donald Gaines said bluntly. "Otherwise what reason would you have to need to speak with Cole? Or does the police department make it a habit of informing crime victims when the people who targeted them are killed?"

"They're just pursuing every lead possible," Madison said quickly again before Marcus could respond.

Without moving his head, Gaines slid his gaze toward Madison for the briefest of moments. "I believe I asked the *detective*."

Though he hadn't raised his voice, the words were as effective as a slap, and even Regina felt the sting of them. She glanced at Madison in time to see him recoil slightly, unable to keep the reaction completely off his face, along with a noticeable trace of nervousness as his eyes shifted between Marcus and Gaines. The way his lips twitched, Regina could tell he wanted to say something, and barely managed to contain himself. She quickly came to two conclusions: Donald Gaines didn't like his son-in-law much, and Cole Madison didn't want his wife and father-in-law to know the specific reason for their visit. That was why he'd interjected, and why he could hardly keep himself from doing so now.

Gaines's stare had returned to Marcus, who met it calmly, unwavering. Regina suspected many people would be intimidated in the face of Gaines's arrogant appraisal. She noticed with some satisfaction that Marcus appeared completely unfazed.

"Your son-in-law is correct, Mr. Gaines," Marcus said. "We are still in the early stages of the investigation and simply exploring all possibilities."

Regina waited for him to bring up the specific business that had brought them here. He didn't, simply staring Gaines down.

It was Tracy Madison who spoke next. "Well, if that man was murdered, I imagine our robbery was only part of the criminal activity he was involved in. He must have crossed all kinds of unsavory characters. And to think Cole wasn't even certain he wanted to press charges."

"But you did?" Regina had to ask.

The woman smiled thinly. "I've never responded well to people trying to take something of mine. I lost some very expensive pieces, not to mention several family heirlooms, in the robbery. If he was guilty, I saw no reason to let him get away with it."

"And you thought he was guilty?"

Tracy blinked at her. "Well, of course. The police arrested him, didn't they?"

"And after he was released?"

She shrugged. "I believe we were told that the case wasn't strong enough, there wasn't enough evidence, something like that. It doesn't mean he was innocent, just that they couldn't prove it." She summoned a smile. "Now, are you done with my husband, detectives? The three of us have lunch reservations and I'm afraid they won't hold the table if we're too tardy. It's hard enough as it is to get Cole to try a new place. If he had his way he'd never go anywhere but Parsons Steakhouse down the street."

The words were spoken with charm, but were wholly insincere. Regina had a feeling that these three could buy and sell any restaurant they wanted several times over. No establishment would dare to give their table away. It was simply a polite way of dismissing them.

"I think that should do it for now," Marcus said. "Thank you for your time, Mr. Madison." He nodded to the others in turn. "Sir. Ma'am."

"Detective," Gaines acknowledged, his eyes never leaving Marcus's until he and Regina turned to leave.

They quickly made their way out of the office and back to the reception area. There were several people in the elevator when they entered, so they remained silent, both checking their phones and thumbing through their missed calls and messages, until they reached the garage and were back in Marcus's car.

"Interesting people," Regina mused as she fastened her seatbelt.

"You can say that again," Marcus muttered. "I'm glad I don't have to sit at that table and have lunch with them."

"You didn't tell Tracy Madison or her father

what really brought us there. You didn't want them to know?"

"I didn't feel like telling Donald Gaines anything," he admitted, starting the engine. "But it was more like *Madison* didn't want them to know. Which meant it was worth keeping it to myself until I have the guy alone without his family in the way to create a scene or get him to clam up. Knowing he wants to keep it from them tells me all I need to know anyway."

"That he's the one who sent the man to Jeremy and Lauren's house," she said. Marcus glanced at her in surprise, and she shrugged. "I noticed, too. And the only reason he could possibly want to keep them from learning about the car is if he knows who sent it and doesn't want them to, most likely because he's the one who did."

"So we're back to the original question: why?"

"And why didn't Madison want to press charges against Jeremy?"

Marcus turned to back out of the space. "I need more background on Cole Madison and his family. In the meantime, let's talk to Eric Howard. I had somebody run a check when I called to get the results on the plate on that car at Lauren Decker's. They got back to me with an address. Maybe he can shine some light on a possible connection between Decker and the Madisons."

He must have been distracted, because he'd automatically included her without thinking about it. Regina wasn't about to point it out to him. She wanted to hear what Eric Howard had to say, too. "Sounds good to me."

A minute later, Marcus pulled out of the garage and onto the street. They were approaching the front of the building they'd just left, the traffic moving slowly, when Regina saw the car. It was idling in front of the building in a marked loading zone. A man standing on the driver's side leaned down toward the window, most likely speaking to the driver. The model of the vehicle was familiar, but it was the first three letters of the license plate—GFS—that made it more than that. Gaines Financial Services?

Then the driver leaned forward to say something to the man outside the vehicle, his face plainly visible for a moment.

The man behind the wheel was the same man who'd been at Lauren Decker's house.

"Marcus, is that—"

"Yes," he said, clearly having seen what she had. "It sure is."

Before he could react, the man standing outside suddenly walked away from the car. Moments later, the vehicle pulled forward, merging into traffic several cars in front of theirs, until she couldn't see it any longer.

"Are you going to follow him?"

Marcus opened his mouth to respond, then closed it again, craning his head to the left. Regina matched the motion to see what he was looking at, just in time to see the car changing lanes again, moving into the one next to theirs.

Marcus checked over his shoulder to see if there was any way he could get into the other lane. Regina automatically did the same.

It didn't look like it. Traffic was too tight.

She glanced back at the man's vehicle, and saw to her dismay that he was turning left at the intersection up ahead. There was no way they'd catch up with him.

Marcus didn't even try. As their lane began moving again, he swung right, pulling into the space the driver had exited in front of the building.

Switching on his hazard lights, Marcus stepped from the vehicle. Regina scrambled to do the same.

They were parked behind the same car

the other driver had been. The man the other driver had been speaking to was standing beside it. It was a town car, no doubt his own vehicle.

"Excuse me," Marcus said, approaching the man. "Can I ask who it was you were speaking to in that car that just drove away?"

The man, who was in his fifties and dressed in a suit just like the other man had been, sent Marcus a suspicious glance. "Who's asking?"

Marcus produced his badge. "Police."

The man's eyes widened. "That was Adrian Moore. He's Mr. Madison's driver."

"And you are?"

"Tom Rainer. I drive Mr. Gaines."

"What were the two of you talking about?"

"I was just confirming for him that he wouldn't be needed. I'm here to pick up Mr. Gaines and Mr. and Mrs. Madison to drive them to lunch."

"Are the two of you friends?"

Tom Rainer briefly made a face of distaste that said what he thought of that idea. "Not really. We seldom see each other. The only place we ever talk is right here, when we happen to be waiting for Mr. Gaines and Mr. Madison at the same time, and then only about that." From his tone, even that was more than he cared to speak with the man.

"How long has he worked for Mr. Madison?"

Rainer appeared to think about it. "Four years, I believe."

"Did Moore happen to mention where he was this morning?"

"No."

"You wouldn't happen to know a Jeremy Decker, would you?"

The man's confusion seemed genuine enough. "No."

"Ever heard the name?"

"No."

"What about Lauren Decker?"

"No."

"All right," Marcus said finally. "Thank you for your time."

The man gave him a wary nod. Marcus and Regina turned away and moved quickly back to Marcus's vehicle.

Moments later, they pulled back into traffic. "So Madison sent his driver to the Deckers," Regina said. "But why?"

"I'd say Mr. Moore's job responsibilities include more than just driving," Marcus replied. "I'd be interested in finding out exactly what else he does for Madison. At least we have a name now. It's a start. Let's see if Eric Howard can fill us in on a connection we're missing."

Chapter Six

Eric Howard lived in the same neighborhood as Lauren Decker, not that far from her house. Marcus had to believe the young woman was aware of that. It made him wonder what else she was hiding. He could only hope Howard could shine some light on that.

Not surprisingly for the middle of a weekday, the man wasn't home. A neighbor informed them he worked at an autobody shop not far from there.

They had no trouble finding it. The shop was decently sized for an independent operation, with three bays on prime streetfront property. Spotting movement in one of the openings, he and Regina headed toward it. An older man with a shock of white hair looked up from beneath a car hoisted in the air as they entered.

"Hello," Marcus said, producing his badge

and identifying himself. "We're looking for Eric Howard."

The man eyed them warily. "He in some kind of trouble?"

"Not at all," Regina said with a smile. "We'd just like to speak with him about a friend of his."

"Jeremy Decker," the man said with a nod.

"How'd you know?" Regina asked.

"Heard what happened to him. And there's only one of Eric's friends I can think of that the police would be interested in. Eric's out at lunch. He should be back in another half hour." Without asking if they wanted to wait or uttering another word, he turned away and went back to his work.

"Well, we know he's not home," Marcus said. "Wherever he went for lunch, it wasn't there. Our best move would be to come back at one."

"I guess that means we have a half hour to kill," Regina noted. "Lunch doesn't sound like a bad idea. I actually haven't eaten anything today. Or last night, come to think of it. I think I saw a sandwich shop down the street."

Her words caught him off-guard, more than they should, a small voice in the back of his mind acknowledged. It didn't stop him from staring at her. "You want to have lunch... together?"

One of those slow-burning smiles he was starting to recognize—the corners of her mouth quirking, her eyes sparkling with humor—lit her face. "Don't worry, Marcus. I can pay for myself. And you don't have to eat anything, but I do. I promise I'll be better lunch company than Gaines and the Madisons."

Her easy tone made him seem foolish for being surprised, and made it impossible to say no. There was no reasonable basis to do it anyway, none that he could admit to at least.

"All right," he said roughly. "Let's grab some lunch."

"So how long have you been in Homicide?"

Marcus had been about to bite into his sandwich when she asked the question. Raising a brow, he lifted his eyes to her face. "Is this going to be an interrogation, counselor? Do I need a lawyer?"

She smiled tolerantly at him. "Relax, *Detective*. I'm just making conversation. And it's Regina, remember?"

He remembered. He just hadn't agreed to

it. It seemed too personal for someone he was still trying his damnedest to keep some distance from. Still, there was no point not answering. It wasn't anything she couldn't find out on her own if she really wanted to know.

He returned his attention to his sandwich. "Seven years," he muttered before taking a bite.

"You must have been young when you made detective," she said, surprise in her voice.

He shrugged. "I worked hard to get where I am. It's what I've always wanted to do."

"Be a police detective, or a homicide detective in particular?"

"Homicide," he said shortly.

"Interesting. What happened that made you want to be a homicide detective?"

He shot her a glance. "What makes you think something happened?"

"Just a guess," Regina said, pulling a chip from the bag in front of her. "Most people choose their careers for a reason, and I've found it's particularly true for police officers."

"You've spent that much time with police officers?"

Marcus sensed her choosing her words carefully. "Mostly in courtroom situations."

He understood immediately. "You try to figure them out in case you can find something to use against them in court," he said darkly.

"It helps to understand the people involved in a case, on both sides," she said without apology. "Like I said, most people have a reason for what they do. With police officers, sometimes it's a good one, like wanting to help people. But sometimes it's a bad one, like ego or a need for power over others. Or sometimes it's just as simple as a family tradition of service."

"So why are you asking me? Trying to find something to use against me?"

"No," she said, her tone saying the idea was ridiculous. "Whatever happens, I'm not going to be trying this case. Like I said, just making conversation. Besides, I honestly don't think I'd find anything."

The comment surprised him. "Really? You're that sure I'm not in it for the power?"

"I am," she said simply, no hesitation.

"Why?" he asked, genuinely curious.

"I told you, I depend on my instincts. I've had a chance to see you at work. You haven't made any attempts to throw your weight around or exert your authority over others, even when you probably could have. You've been all about the case and the best way of solving it, which I appreciate."

"Maybe I've just been on my best behavior with you around."

She actually appeared to consider it, taking a bite and chewing slowly for a moment, then shook her head. "I don't think so. It doesn't fit. You strike me as someone who's in it for the right reasons."

With another woman he might have thought she was flirting, the compliment simply a come-on, playing to his ego. It might have been accompanied by a playful smile, maybe a wink.

There was none of that with this woman. He knew immediately that she wasn't being coy, she wasn't playing games. She met his eyes with that disarming straightforwardness of hers, the words plain-spoken and true.

Part of him recognized that he should probably feel wary toward this woman. She was a lawyer. She knew how to be convincing, how to manipulate people using only her words, how to get them to reveal things they didn't want to. She could be playing him, even if he didn't know why she would be.

And yet, she wasn't the only one who relied on her instincts, and his were telling him that with this woman, what you see is what you get. She seemed incapable of being anything other than what she was, but then, with a woman like her, what else would she need to be? She had the kind of easy confidence that was rare to find in anybody. It wasn't arrogance. She wasn't going out of her way to seem smug and superior. It was simply an inherent part of who she was, something that came across in her demeanor, a self-assurance that said she knew who she was and was comfortable with herself. He would be lying, if only to himself, if he tried to pretend he didn't find it appealing.

Uncomfortable with the idea, he reached for the only thing he could: the truth, needing the reminder more than ever.

"My sister was murdered," he said roughly. "She was only seventeen. The guy who did it had no business being out of jail at the time, but he was."

There was a pause before she said, "Because a defense attorney got him out."

He gave a short jerk of his head in acknowledgment.

"What happened to him?" she asked.

"Nothing. They never caught him. He got away scot-free."

"And so you chose a career where you could

catch those guilty of crime and ensure they didn't get away with it."

He snorted. "Sounds awfully pat when you put it like that."

"I didn't mean it that way. But it makes sense that you would be drawn to a career in law enforcement. Some who've been touched by crime obviously won't want to be reminded of it, but it's only natural for many who have to want to do something about it as well."

"So you can see why I don't have much use for defense attorneys who don't care what they put back on the street."

She raised her eyebrows. "Is that what you've heard about me? No wonder you don't like me."

"I didn't say that," he said quickly.

"You didn't have to," she said with a gentle smile. "It was pretty clear. I assumed it was simply a police officer's aversion for criminal defense attorneys. I didn't realize there was more to it than that."

He waited for her to continue. She didn't, taking another bite of her sandwich, her eyes drifting shut for the slightest of moments, a soft moan emerging from her throat. Pleasure washed over her face, her expression sending a jolt of energy straight to his groin.

Her eyes opened, then met his. She blinked

at him. "What?" she asked, and he suddenly realized he was staring.

He scrambled to remember what he'd been thinking about. Her lack of anger or defensiveness at the idea that he didn't like defense attorneys. "You're not going to try to defend yourself?"

She blinked again, and he could tell the idea had never occurred to her. "I'm not going to apologize for my job, Marcus. Yes, I do fight hard for my clients. It's why I have my own practice, so I can choose which cases I want to take. If I was in it for the money and didn't care who I defended, I would be at a big firm, taking any case that came my way and raking it in. My bank account would certainly be better off if I did. But justice shouldn't only be for those who can afford it, with the rich getting a different standard of justice than those who don't have a lot of money. Believe it or not, I do have standards and I need to believe in the cases I take. I think that we both know that the police aren't always right. Police officers are people, too, not always good people either, and people make mistakes. Which is why everyone has the right to a defense and deserves to have someone fight for them. And if I can fight for someone who I feel needs it and help them in any way, then I'll do it."

From the passion in her voice, she believed strongly in every word. He would have been surprised if she'd displayed anything else. If she did anything else for a living, he'd probably respect that passion. Hell, part of him still did.

At the same time, he couldn't help but wonder if there wasn't more of a reason for that passion, her earlier words coming back to him. "You say it's only natural for people who've been touched by crime to want to do something about it. From the sound of it, I'm guessing that's true for you, too."

She chuckled lightly. "I walked right into that one, didn't I?" She nodded. "Kurt Bishop's sister was my best friend growing up."

Marcus couldn't keep the reaction off his face. She didn't miss it. "I can see I don't have to explain who that is," she said.

"No," he said grimly, suddenly understanding her passion all too well and wishing he didn't. It made it a hell of a lot harder to dispute what she was saying.

The Kurt Bishop case was an infamous and ugly example of justice gone wrong. It was before his time, but he doubted there was anyone in the police department, not to mention the city, who didn't know it. A teenage girl had been murdered, her wealthy and connected father had been screaming for blood, and the officers on the case had been under heavy pressure to make an arrest. So they'd made one, charging Kurt Bishop, a young man who'd been seen in the area shortly before the murder took place.

Unfortunately for everybody involved, the case against him had required manufacturing a large chunk of the evidence. He had an alibi, one the detectives had leaned on—some said outright threatened—to keep from coming forward. A key piece of physical evidence against him had been planted, while another piece of evidence that would have pointed to the true killer had been conveniently misplaced. As a result, Bishop had been convicted and the detectives on the case had come out looking golden—at least until the truth came out, something that had taken years to happen. Even then it had required a religious conversion on the part of the real killer and a close reevaluation of the DNA evidence. Kurt Bishop had spent more than ten years in prison before he was finally released.

It was an ugly story, one Marcus hated, not just because of the injustice to Kurt Bishop and his family, but because those detectives had made the entire department and everyone on the job look bad, seeming to justify every suspicion people had about whether the police could be trusted. As if the job wasn't hard enough.

"I guess, being so close to the family, you must have heard all about it," he said.

"I didn't need to," Regina said. "I was there the night the police came looking for him. I was sleeping over and even though Kim and I were upstairs we could hear everything. I remember listening to the officers talking to him and his parents. I was only thirteen, but I still knew it wasn't right. The way they spoke to these good people, twisted their words, badgered them, tried to say they'd said things they hadn't. I knew it was wrong. But there was no one to stop them. I'm sure none of the Bishops thought to ask for an attorney. People like to think that only the guilty ask for attorneys, that innocent people don't need them. Except I think we both know that's not true. Everybody needs somebody to fight for them, and not just in legal circumstances. Even after he was arrested, they couldn't afford an attorney, so he was assigned a public defender, someone fresh out of law school with an overburdened caseload who was entirely out of his league. And look what happened."

She shook her head. "At first, I thought I would be the one to prove Kurt was innocent.

Luckily it didn't take that long, and the conviction was overturned while I was in law school. But I promised myself no one else would be caught in those circumstances if there was anything I could do about it."

The hell of it was, Marcus couldn't deny anything she was saying, especially when she had Kurt Bishop to offer as part of her argument. He knew a lot of defense attorneys did some good and helped people who needed it, people who might not get a fair shake without them. And though he hated admitting it, even to himself, he knew there were some cops who just weren't very good at their jobs or who misused the public trust placed in them. In theory, he could recognize what defense attorneys did and the role they played.

He just couldn't get involved with one.

It didn't matter that Regina Garrett was the first woman to capture his attention in a very long time, and more than he could ever remember. It didn't matter that he was actually starting to like her, no matter how much he didn't want to and hadn't thought he would. It didn't even matter that, more than that, he was starting to respect her. He'd hated the idea that he could be this attracted to a woman without ethics, without morals, who had no qualms about putting bad guys back on the street, no matter what she had to do. But the more time he spent with her, the more he could see that wasn't who she was. And yet it still didn't matter.

Because it wasn't about the innocent people she helped. It was about the guilty ones. If there was even one person who was out on the street who shouldn't be, who hurt someone because she made it possible, it was one too many. For all he knew, the lawyer who'd gotten Kay's murderer out in time to kill her had represented only one truly bad guy. Maybe every other client he'd had had been squeaky clean and completely innocent, and maybe every other action he'd ever taken had been on the side of the angels. It didn't seem likely—anyone who would take the case of a man with the background of Kay's killer couldn't have any reservations about representing similar types—but it was possible. It wouldn't matter. Because he'd still gotten that one guy off, still taken the case of somebody who had no business being on the street and made it possible for him to kill again. No amount of good could ever make up for that. And the same was true with her.

He knew it probably wasn't fair. It probably

wasn't reasonable. He wasn't saying it was, even to himself. It was simply the way it was.

He lost enough sleep at night over the bad guys who were on the streets because he hadn't been able to put them away. He couldn't lose any more over the ones who were out there because of her.

Not that he could say any of that. Regina was watching him, waiting for his response. There was nothing he could say that would serve any purpose.

He finally said, "We should hurry up and finish if we're going to get back to the garage by one."

She simply nodded, though he didn't miss the flash of disappointment that passed over her face before she returned her attention to her meal.

He did the same. Being around this woman had been like playing with fire from the moment he'd first seen her. He could only hope the cold hard truth had finally doused that particular flame.

But as he focused on the remains of his sandwich, not looking at her, he still felt her there, as strongly as ever, and knew it wasn't going to be that easy.

THEY MADE IT BACK to the garage shortly after one. Eric Howard should be back from lunch by now.

Marcus spotted him as soon as they entered the garage, recognizing him from the photo they'd seen just a few hours earlier. Obviously the man was a little older than he'd been when the photograph was taken, now in his mid-twenties as Jeremy Decker had been. He remained a tall, lean man, now dressed in a work uniform with slight grease stains on the shirt.

At Marcus and Regina's arrival, the man they'd spoken to earlier called out Howard's name, then nudged his chin toward them when he looked up. Grimacing, Howard wiped his hands on his uniform and headed toward them.

"You the folks who were looking for me earlier?"

"Yes," Marcus said. "Detective Marcus Waters. This is Regina Garrett. She was Jeremy Decker's defense attorney. I don't know if you've heard yet what happened to him."

The man nodded tersely. "I heard."

"We were hoping to speak with you about him, see if there's anything you can tell us that can help us figure out who's responsible for his death."

Eric Howard eyed him, skepticism clearly written in the narrowing of his eyes and downward tilt of his mouth. "Sure, why not? I just hope you're better at your job than the cops who arrested him in the first place."

He stepped outside and past them, leading them to a quiet spot out of the way where they were unlikely to be overheard.

When he turned around to face them, Marcus spoke again. "I take it you believe he was innocent of the charges against him."

"I know he was."

"Did he tell you that?"

"He didn't have to. I knew Jeremy since we were kids. He never did a bad thing in his whole life."

"Did he offer any explanation for his whereabouts at the house, why his fingerprints were at the scene?"

Howard shook his head. "I haven't spoken to Jeremy since before he was arrested. He didn't want to see me when he was in jail, and I didn't see him after he got out."

"He didn't come to see you?"

"No. I stopped by the house, but Lauren said he was out. I told her to have him call me, but he never did."

"Didn't that seem strange to you?" Regina asked. "I was under the impression the two of you were close."

"I thought we were, too. I didn't take it personally. I'm sure he was embarrassed by what happened, maybe needed time to get used to being back in the real world."

"Can you think of anyone else he might have contacted or gone to see?" Marcus asked.

"Sure I can. But none of them heard from him, either. I asked around."

"If he was behaving so strangely, maybe he'd changed. Maybe he'd become the kind of person who would do a bad thing."

"No way. Jeremy was the most upright guy I ever met in my life. His sister was always the wild one in the family."

"Lauren?" Regina asked, the surprise in her voice mirroring Marcus's own.

"Yeah. Ever since high school, she was always running around and getting into trouble, stirring up things, hooking up with the wrong guys. Jeremy always tried to do right by her, and it wasn't easy. Last year he said she was dating Troy Lewis, this real lowlife." He shook his head. "The guy's nothing but trouble. I guess she finally figured that out for herself, since Jeremy said they broke up. Not before Troy got her pregnant though."

So that was who the father of Lauren's baby was. "You say he's nothing but trouble," Marcus said. "What kind of trouble?"

"You tell me. You're the cop. The guy's had plenty of run-ins with the police, the way I hear it."

"I'll look into it," Marcus promised. "Do you know of any connection between Jeremy and Cole and Tracy Madison, other than the burglary?"

"No."

"What about Lauren?" Regina asked.

"No. I've never heard those names before."

"What about Adrian Moore?"

"No."

"All right," Marcus said. "Thank you, Mr. Howard. You've been very helpful."

The man shot him a pointed look. "Just find out who did this. Jeremy was a good guy. He didn't deserve this." With that, he turned and went back to the garage.

Marcus and Regina headed in the opposite direction toward where Marcus had parked his car on the street. "This could be what we were looking for," Regina said. "It's the first connection we've found between Jeremy and someone with a criminal background."

"It's certainly worth looking into further. Did Decker tell you anything about this Lewis?"

"No, he never mentioned the name. I didn't even know who the father of Lauren's baby was."

"Well, if Lewis has the kind of criminal background Howard seems to think he does, it could explain how Decker was roped into a burglary. There could have been some kind of coercion involved, if Lewis used Lauren or the baby, or both, to force Decker to participate."

"Or Jeremy could have heard about what Lewis was doing and tried to stop him," Regina suggested.

He sent her an amused look. "Still determined to believe Decker was innocent, are you?"

"Until it's proven otherwise."

They finally reached his car. Marcus checked his watch. "I need to get back to the station. I've been gone a lot longer than I thought I would. I'll drop you off at your house."

She stopped and looked at him over the top of the car. "What about Lewis?"

"I'll run a background check and get an address."

"And you'll let me know what you find?"

He hesitated. This was it, his chance to put an end to her active involvement in the case. There was no reason for her to continue. They'd reached the point where she'd likely provided as much information as she could, which meant her usefulness and only reason to be involved no longer applied. It was for the best, both in terms of her safety and for him personally.

That didn't mean he didn't feel a faint trace of disappointment about it, one he quickly shook off.

"I will inform you if there are any breaks in the case," he said carefully. It was a nice promise, one which actually promised nothing. It all depended on the definition of "break." If he had his way, it meant when they had a suspect in custody, or maybe when charges were filed.

Of course, he didn't kid himself into thinking she'd give up that easily. He braced himself for her response, ready for the argument sure to follow.

She stared at him for a moment, then slowly smiled. "Thank you," she said. "I would appreciate it." Without another word, she pulled the door open and climbed in.

Closing his eyes, Marcus choked back a groan. The "thank you" sounded believable enough, but he didn't buy it for a second.

She was up to something. He almost had to admire her determination.

Even as he had to dread whatever she was planning to do next.

Chapter Seven

"Lynn, it's Regina."

A loud snort greeted the announcement. "Please tell me you're not calling me from the Caribbean."

"I'm not calling you from the Caribbean," Regina deadpanned. "I'm calling you from my car."

This time she was rewarded with a laugh. "Of course you are. I knew you couldn't take a vacation."

"The decision was out of my hands. I don't know if you heard, but one of my clients was murdered last night."

Her investigator instantly sobered. "No, I hadn't. Who?"

"Jeremy Decker. He was parked in his car outside my office building. I found his body."

"Oh, Reg. Are you okay?"

"I'm hanging in there. And now I need some information."

"Anything you need," Lynn said. "That's what I'm here for."

"I need background on some people involved in the case, everything you can find." She rattled off every name that had come up so far—Lauren, both Madisons, Gaines, Moore, Howard, Lewis. "Also, we need to dig deeper into any possible connections between Jeremy and the Madisons. If there's any way he could have been connected to them prior to the robbery, I need to know about it."

"You got it."

"And I know it goes without saying, but I need everything ASAP."

"Not a problem. Most of the rest of the world *is* on vacation. My time is yours."

"Guess it's a good thing for me you don't know how to take a vacation, either."

"Hey, workaholics keep the world running."

Regina laughed. "Thanks, Lynn."

Satisfied, Regina ended the call and focused on the road. After Marcus had dropped her off at home, she'd realized she'd failed to do the one thing she'd intended that morning— go to her office and read through her file on

Jeremy's case. If there was anything in it, she needed to know, the sooner the better.

It was just starting to get dark, not quite rush hour yet. With any luck, she would be able to get in and out of her office and back on the road before the full rush, or what passed for it at this time of year, hit.

She'd known that Marcus was telling her none-too-subtly that her involvement in the case had come to an end as far as he was concerned. She'd also known she really couldn't argue the point. She wasn't a cop. She'd told him as much as she honestly believed she knew. She'd been fortunate to talk her way into participating as much as she had.

Of course, if he also thought she was going to sit by and do nothing while Jeremy's killer was out there, a killer who'd made a clear threat against her, then he was a fool.

Judging from the suspicious looks he'd been giving her on the drive back to her house, most likely caused by the fact that she hadn't argued, he *wasn't* that much of a fool, she thought with a smile.

In a way she should be grateful. After feeling so unsettled around him all day, she should be happy for the chance to get away from him for a while and regain her senses. But when he'd called an end to their temporary partnership, she hadn't been relieved. She'd been disappointed. Mostly because he was trying to stop her involvement in the case, but also, yes, because it meant they were going to be saying goodbye, even if she only intended for it to be temporary.

At their impromptu lunch, she'd tried to get a better sense of who he was, needing a better explanation for her strong response toward him, hoping for a reason why it shouldn't exist. Instead, she'd only come away liking him more. It seemed strange now that she knew he had a specific reason for disliking criminal defense attorneys, which meant nothing was ever likely to happen between them. And yet, she'd just found herself hoping there was a way there could be.

He was smart and undeniably quick, as she'd learned in their conversations, some of the fast exchanges between them giving her a rush of exhilaration. She'd meant what she'd told him—she did believe he was a good cop who was in it for the right reasons, and everything she'd seen told her he was principled and good at his job. And there was no denying his obvious physical appeal. Even as she thought it, the image of the man himself rose in her mind, and she felt her heart pick up speed again.

One day, an irritatingly logical voice in the back of her head intoned. *You've known him one day.* Less than that, really. It was far too soon to be this drawn to a man she'd just met, this interested. This kind of immediate attraction didn't happen in real life, not on this level. At least it had never happened to her. She couldn't believe it seemed to be happening now.

Minutes later, she finally arrived on the street where her building was located. She deliberately ignored the spot where Jeremy's car had been parked the night before, hardly needing the reminder. Pulling into the garage, she took the elevator up to her floor.

Keys in hand, she moved quickly to her suite and unlocked the door. Cold air struck her as soon as she stepped into the room, raising goose bumps on her skin and making her shiver. She'd turned the thermostat down before leaving yesterday, rather than heat an empty office for several weeks. Good thing she didn't intend to stay long.

The light switch was just inside the door. She flipped on one set of lights, leaving half the room in shadow. She was about to reach back and close the door when she heard a scrambling sound. There was no time to process it. A heartbeat later, a weight suddenly slammed into her back, knocking her off her feet. She tumbled forward, a scream bursting from her throat. She threw her hands out to break her fall. They didn't do much to protect her from the impact as she crashed to the carpet and skidded forward, pain erupting in her hands and arms.

She caught a flash of motion out of the corner of her eye. Instinct made her jerk her head in that direction, just in time to see a figure dressed entirely in black, head covered in a wool cap, darting out the door.

"Hey!" The yell came out on its own, exploding from her mouth. Even as she said it, she scrambled to get back on her feet, her hands burning, her muscles aching from the effort. The sound of footsteps pounding down the hall fired her determination, anger overshadowing the pain. The intruder was getting away. She couldn't let it happen. She had to go after him.

She finally managed to stumble to the door, only to hear the sound of the stairwell door at the far end of the hall slamming against the wall. She lunged forward, moving faster with every step.

By the time she got there, the stairwell door had already swung shut again. She shoved through it, then skidded to a halt at the top of the stairs, her ears telling her the truth before she went any farther. The only footsteps she heard were far away, likely almost at the bottom of the stairs by now. There was no way she could catch up.

Damn it.

Shoulders sagging, she sucked in a breath and tried to calm her heartbeat. Anger churned in her gut as the full implications of what had just happened settled in. Someone had broken into her office, basically attacked her in their attempt to get away. She had a feeling she should feel violated, but mostly she felt ticked off. She'd never been burglarized before, never had any home she'd lived in or any workplace broken into. This building may not be the most high-security structure, but she'd never felt less than safe here. Why would someone break into her office of all places?

And just like that, she knew.

Needing to see for herself, she spun on her heel and headed back down the hall. As soon as she reached her suite, she moved through the reception area toward the inner office where her current files were. Jeremy's should be in there since she'd been looking at it so recently.

One glance was all it took to confirm her suspicion.

Jeremy's file was gone.

"I SHOULD HAVE COME back last night," Regina said with barely concealed anger, all of it clearly directed at herself. "If I had come up after we got back from talking to Lauren, I could have picked up the file then and this wouldn't have happened."

"They still would have broken in," Marcus pointed out. They stood in the reception area of her office, out of earshot of the locksmith who knelt at the door. From the marks on it, it appeared the intruder had picked the locks to get in. Naturally, she'd decided to have them changed.

"But they wouldn't have gotten away with the file."

"And you wouldn't have been attacked," he said, a far more important fact as far as he was concerned.

She waved a hand. "I'm fine. The file is what matters."

Barely swallowing his impatience, he almost said, *To hell with the file*. He bit back the words, knowing he'd have to explain the strange comment to her—and himself.

He'd come as soon as she'd called, anger

and adrenaline making him drop what he'd been doing on the spot to rush to her office. Not until he'd seen her in the flesh had the tension knotting in his chest started to loosen. He knew the reaction hadn't made any sense. She'd sounded fine on the phone and obviously been capable of making the call in the first place. But hearing her voice was a lot different from seeing her in person and confirming it for himself, and he wouldn't have put it past her to put on a strong front over the phone.

Even now, he couldn't keep from studying her, seeking any signs of injury. She'd said the intruder had slammed into her and knocked her to the floor, an idea that filled him with fresh anger just thinking about it. She was dressed as she'd been earlier that day, still wearing her coat despite being indoors, and her clothes didn't appear to be torn or bloodied. Any cuts or bruises she may have suffered weren't immediately visible, most likely covered by her clothing. If she had sustained any injuries, she wasn't admitting to them. Not that he would expect her to. From the moment he'd arrived, she'd dismissed the assault like it was nothing, caring only about the file.

He couldn't do the same, guilt nagging too heavily at him. He should have anticipated this would happen, should have stuck by her, just in case. They'd known she was a target, that someone was afraid of what she knew. He should have considered that the killer would want to know what was in her files. He might have if he'd known she was planning on coming back here. But he hadn't, and he had no one to blame for that but himself. He'd been so focused on his own concerns, needing to spend some time away from her and create some distance between them, he hadn't thought about what might happen after he left her.

It was a mistake he wouldn't make again.

"You'd just found a dead body," Marcus said reasonably. "It was only natural to want to try to deal with that instead of jumping back into the case."

"Natural, maybe. But not smart."

He decided to drop it. She wasn't in a mood to be convinced or made to feel better, so there wasn't much use arguing the point. "You're sure nothing else was taken?"

"Not that I can tell. I'll have to do an inventory of my files just in case anything else is missing." Her weary tone made it clear how much she was looking forward to that. "I doubt anything is. I think we both know what they were after."

"They really want to know what you know, even if it's something you don't realize you know."

She nodded. "That's what I figured."

"What exactly was in the file? Everything you had, or is there anything left?"

"The most important things in there, the only things I can't replicate, were my handwritten notes. I try to transcribe my notes into a computer file so I have everything available electronically, but I tend to clean them up during the process so they're more ordered. The handwritten notes contain everything I jotted down, every little notation I made or thought I had at the time, things that may not have made it into the electronic file. I was hoping there was something in there that might help, something I didn't realize was important and wouldn't have transcribed that might mean something to me now."

"There's no point worrying about it. You'll just have to work off what you have. You never know. What you're looking for might be in your electronic file and you might not even know it."

"I hope you're right," she murmured, her skepticism clear.

"All done," the locksmith said. Marcus turned to see the man had risen. Regina stepped away from Marcus to speak with the man, quickly settling the bill and accepting a receipt and the new keys. "Thank you for coming so quickly. I really appreciate it."

"No problem," he said, bending down to pick up his toolbox. "Good night. Happy holidays."

"Happy holidays," Regina echoed. Understandably enough, there was a noticeable lack of holiday cheer in her voice. The anger had faded as well, leaving only frustration and that hint of weariness. It didn't show on her face, her expression too stubborn to reveal anything else, but it was evident in the slump of her shoulders that she was tired. Looking at her, he couldn't keep from frowning. No matter how much she claimed to be fine, it had been a long day, and she'd been through a lot in the past twenty-four hours. She needed to get out of here. She needed to get some rest.

"Are you done here?" he asked.

"I think so."

"Where are you parked?"

"In the garage."

"I'll follow you home."

She looked up at him, her brow furrowing. "You don't have to do that."

"Yeah, I do," he said simply. He waited for her to object further and say it wasn't necessary, preparing himself for an argument he fully intended to win.

Surprisingly enough, she didn't protest further. She simply gave a vague nod and said, "All right. Let me just make sure everything's closed up. For all the good it did last time."

The fact that she didn't argue bothered him just as much as it had earlier when he'd dropped her off at her house. This time it wasn't suspicion, but concern that had him narrowing his eyes and studying her closer.

She did seem fine physically. Emotionally was another matter. Even if she wouldn't admit it, even if she didn't realize it, having somebody ambush her in the dark had to have affected her, even subconsciously. He wasn't even the one who'd been attacked, and it had affected him. Thinking about it, picturing it, sent anger and guilt spiking through him, and he grimaced.

He hadn't needed any more incentive to solve this case, but he had it anyway. He was going to get this guy, and the bastard was never going to get this close to Regina again.

Chapter Eight

True to his word, Marcus stayed right behind her the entire drive back to her house. Regina really hadn't thought it necessary. Yet somehow his insistence didn't strike her as high-handed. If anything, his clear concern had seemed rather comforting, just as his presence behind her did on the drive.

Arriving at her house, he pulled into the driveway behind her car. She climbed out, intending to walk back to his vehicle to say thank you before he left. But he was already leaving his car as well, walking forward to join her between the two sedans.

He wasn't looking at her, instead studying her house through narrowed eyes. It was after six, and night had fallen a while ago. She hadn't left any lights on when she'd left, not intending to be gone so long. The building was shrouded in darkness. "Is there somewhere else you can stay?" he asked, surprising her.

"Why?"

"I'm not sure it's a good idea for you to stay here alone."

"I'll be fine. I was alone last night and nothing happened."

"Nothing but someone leaving a tongue on your doorstep."

Inwardly, she shuddered at the reminder, though she didn't let the reaction show. "Yes, *outside*. They didn't try to break in."

"They didn't break into your office yesterday, either. That didn't stop them from doing it today."

"When they thought I wasn't there," she pointed out with a smile. "I'm sure I'll be fine. It'll be a lot harder for them to pick the locks on my house out in the open."

His frown didn't ease, and she realized he was genuinely concerned. She knew it probably wasn't personal. He'd likely feel the same way about anyone involved in one of his cases who'd dealt with the types of circumstances she had. But in spite of herself, she couldn't help but feel a little touched at his worry on her behalf.

"Do you want me to check the house, make

sure everything's okay and there aren't any nasty surprises waiting for you?"

Her first instinct was to brush off the suggestion. But his mention of nasty surprises brought back some of the others she'd faced in the past twenty-four hours, and this time she couldn't quite manage to suppress the shiver that worked its way down her spine.

"All right," she said, reaching in her purse for her keys. "Thank you."

He held his hand out for the keys. She reached out and placed them in it, her fingertips grazing the heel of his palm. A completely unexpected jolt shot through her, an undeniable spark of awareness. Her eyes flew to his, and from the sudden widening of his eyes she knew he'd felt it, too.

It occurred to her this was the first time they'd ever touched. It was almost hard to believe, given how attuned to him she'd been all this time, feeling his presence as closely as an actual caress against her skin. At least that was how it had seemed. That brief taste of true contact verified they hadn't come close to actually touching until now, the real thing only making her hungry for more.

"Thanks," he murmured, dropping his hand to his side. Lowering his eyes, he started up the front path.

She followed him to the door, watching as he unlocked it and pushed it open. "There's a switch just inside the door," she said.

He flipped it, and the lights in the living room flared on. From what she could see over his shoulder, everything looked fine. He must have thought so, too, because he said, "I'll be right back." Drawing his weapon, he proceeded into the house.

Ready to get in out of the cold, Regina stepped inside, remaining in the entryway. The house was quiet; she couldn't even hear him moving through the building. Observing the peaceful stillness, it seemed impossible that anything could be wrong here, and she almost felt foolish for having him go to the trouble of checking. But then, it had been quiet at first in her office as well, and that hadn't been the result of a lack of danger. Instead, it had only meant an intruder was remaining quiet before acting, only that last-second sound providing a warning, when it was too late. Remembering that, it seemed entirely too possible that the silence in the house was simply concealing someone too clever to make a sound, someone who could be lurking in her own home…

She shuddered, folding her arms over her chest and rubbing her arms. No, considering what had happened hours earlier, a little extra caution couldn't hurt.

A gust of wind blew past her, pulling at her coat and blasting through the layers of clothes. She suddenly realized how exposed she was standing there in the open doorway.

Glancing behind her, Regina surveyed the street. The roadway was clear, no vehicles traveling down it, no strange cars parked along the curb. The neighborhood remained quiet and serene, every house on the block aglow with holiday lights.

Rather than fill her with seasonal cheer, the festive scene only made her sad, the cheerfulness of the other houses emphasizing how dark and quiet hers was. Unlike her, all her neighbors were safe and snug in their homes, their holidays untainted by violence or crime. She tried to remember what that felt like. She almost couldn't, even after only a day of this.

"All clear."

She started at the sound of his voice, turning to find Marcus coming down the stairs. His eyes moved past her to the door. "Everything all right down here?"

"Yes. Why?"

"You were staring out that door even before

I went upstairs. I thought you might have spotted something."

"No." She forced a smile. "Just admiring the view."

"Well, everything looks fine. Doors and windows are all locked tight and nothing seems out of place as far as I can tell."

"Thank you. I really appreciate it. And I'm sorry to have taken up so much of your time. I'm sure you have other places to be, especially with how crazy this time of the year is."

He gave a loose shrug, those broad shoulders barely moving. "Don't worry about it. You're not keeping me away from anything."

Or anyone? she wondered, experiencing a ridiculous flicker of hope. Not that she had any business asking such a thing.

So she kept her tone light. "No holiday parties? No last-minute shopping to take care of?"

"No, nothing like that. Shopping's pretty easy when you don't have anybody to buy for."

That ridiculous lightness in her chest instantly turned heavy. "No one? No family?"

"No. Losing my sister pretty much killed my parents. My mother died a few years later, my dad a few years after that. I'm the only one who's left."

"What are you doing for Christmas?" she asked before she could think better of it.

"Probably just a turkey sandwich and whatever NBA game's on. I'm lucky to have the day off."

The very idea of him, alone in a house or an apartment—she didn't even know where he lived—with just a sandwich and a basketball game, struck her as terribly wrong. How was that possible? He was so great, yet he was going to be just as alone as she was. Strange that they should have that in common.

He must have noticed something in her expression, because he said, "It's okay." The corners of his mouth lifted in a small smile. "It's not that bad. Nothing to be sad about."

"I wasn't," she fibbed. "I was just thinking that I can relate, at least to the being alone part."

"No family either?"

"No. I never had any brothers and sisters. My father died when I was twelve, my mother five years ago."

"So this trip you were taking, it was by yourself?"

"Yeah," she admitted. "I figured as long as I was going to be on my own I might as well be in a place with better weather and nicer scenery. I mean, I have friends who would gladly have me over, but it's hard not to feel out of place spending the holiday with somebody else's family."

"I know how that is." His smile turned rueful. "Especially if you show up and find out they have somebody they want you to meet."

"Oh, God," Regina groaned. "There's nothing worse than a surprise setup."

"And you can't just leave so you're stuck avoiding the other person—or avoiding each other—for the next several hours."

"Believe me, I've been there," Regina chuckled. "So I take it there's nobody special in your life at the moment either?"

"No," he said, instantly causing the lightness to return. "I haven't met a woman who'd be willing to put up with my job and everything it involves. Haven't met anybody I'd want to ask to put up with it, either, to be honest."

"You've never been married?"

"Only to the job," he said with a small grin. "You?"

She returned the smile. "Same. It's not what I expected to happen, but it's just how things worked out. It's not easy to meet a good man in my line of work."

"I'm sure you've met plenty of police officers," he said lightly, and she realized he was teasing her.

"Most of the officers I've encountered don't really care for me. I thought we covered that," she said wryly.

"Maybe they just needed a chance to get to know you."

"Maybe. I haven't met all that many who wanted to try."

"Their loss."

The comment sent a flush of pleasure to her cheeks. She could tell he hadn't just been trying to be nice. Indeed, she watched as his eyes widened slightly in surprise. It was clear he hadn't intended to say it, hadn't thought about it at all. He'd simply said what he was thinking, the response immediate and honest, which meant he really did mean it.

He cleared his throat. "I should go."

"Right."

She turned to let him move past her to the door. He stepped forward to do so, but stopped halfway, until he was standing in front of her, the two of them just inside the doorway, their bodies incredibly close.

He'd had his head lowered slightly when

he started by. When he stopped, he opened his mouth, evidently about to say something, and raised his head. It was only then that he seemed to notice just how close they were now standing. His entire body went very still, his eyes scanning over her face, meeting her eyes, lingering at her mouth.

And for a brief moment, she thought he was about to kiss her.

She didn't need to wait for it. She could kiss him. They were standing close enough that all she would really need to do was lean forward and push up on her toes.

Something held her in place. She did need to wait for it, needed to know that she wasn't imagining what she thought she felt between them, that he felt it too and was willing to act on it despite his admitted aversion to her career. If it was going to happen, he would have to make it happen. And more than anything, she wanted him to make it happen.

Then the moment passed.

Dropping his head, he nodded tightly. "Good night, then." With that, he turned and moved outside.

"Good night," she echoed faintly.

She used a shaky hand to push the door shut, then sagged back against the solid surface, releasing a long, uneven breath.

Well, that answered that.

She swallowed the disappointment that rose in her throat, thankful she hadn't made a fool of herself. Evidently what she thought she'd sensed between them was entirely one-sided. He really wasn't interested. Better that she know for sure now so she could try to start getting past whatever she was feeling before it got out of control.

Too bad she had a feeling it was going to be much easier said than done.

MARCUS WAS HALFWAY TO his vehicle when he stopped. Regina's face remained in the forefront of his mind, not having faded at all from the moment he'd left her. The way she'd looked on her doorstep, her face tilted up toward his, an open, almost hopeful, expression on it, her eyes aglow, her lips slightly parted.

He'd almost kissed her. He'd wanted to kiss her. It made no sense beyond the purely physical. Yes, he wanted her, more than he could ever remember wanting a woman, and that was saying something. His body seemed to burn from the inside out with it. But she was involved in the case, which was a good reason not to risk making things awkward. She was a defense attorney, which was a good reason not to want to have anything to do with her. Not to mention that, after everything she'd been through, she didn't need some guy taking advantage of her weakened emotional state.

Even as he thought the last one, he knew it was a laughable idea. Regina Garrett had to be the most strong-willed woman he'd ever met in his life, and he'd known plenty of those. He had no doubt that she wouldn't let anything happen that she didn't want to. In those last moments, when they'd been standing incredibly close, when all he would have had to do was lean in, she hadn't stepped back.

The memory of it, the way she'd looked in that moment, hovered in his mind as clearly as if she was still standing there in front of him. Her lips parted. Her eyes shining as they stared up into his. The soft hitch of the breath in her throat. She'd stood there, as though she was ready for it, as though she was waiting for it…

And he'd walked away from something they'd both wanted.

Suddenly none of the rest mattered. He didn't have any answers for the other reasons.

He just knew that if he was going to spend the rest of the night thinking about what it would be like to kiss her anyway, he wasn't leaving until he'd experienced the real thing.

REGINA WAS ABOUT TO step into the kitchen when she heard the knock on the door. She stopped and slowly turned back. It had to be Marcus, of course. He wouldn't have had time to return to his car, start the engine and leave yet, and he wouldn't have let someone else approach her door while he was still there, at least not without accompanying them.

Curious, she made her way back to the door. A glance through the window confirmed it was him. He was alone.

She pulled the door open. The porch light shone over him, yet his expression remained unreadable.

"Marcus," she said, simply for lack of anything else. "Did you forget something?"

"Yes," he said. The thickness in his voice sent a tremor rumbling through her, stirring a reaction she thought had died with his departure.

He stepped forward, filling the doorframe, until they were inches apart. The tremor gained intensity, until it felt like a storm was building within her, churning in her belly. He reached down and hooked his forefinger under her chin, lifting her face to his.

She waited, breathless, to see what he would do. Behind him, the holiday lights on her neighbors' homes sparkled in the background like a million multi-colored stars, giving the world, this moment, an unreal, almost magical feel. She knew it should be cold, felt the motion of the wind blowing past and around them, saw their breaths mixing and rising into the air. All she registered was heat, from that small spot where his finger met her chin, the only place where they were touching, from his eyes poring over her face and staring deep into her own.

Then, as though granting her something she'd been waiting an eternity for, he finally lowered his mouth to hers.

Her eyelids drifted shut, and a heartbeat later, their lips met. The first long, slow caress of his mouth against hers was nearly enough to buckle her knees, driving a soft moan to her throat. He worked his warm, firm lips against hers slowly, taking his time, as though savoring each touch, each taste. There was something achingly tender in each deliberate stroke of his mouth over hers. Warmth burst through her chest, spreading through her entire body, until it felt as though every bone was on the verge of melting, her limbs going weak. The kiss was surprisingly gentle, more than she would have expected given the raw strength of the attraction she'd felt building between them, but there was a sureness to it, something that struck a chord of feminine recognition within her that this man knew exactly what he was doing.

They deepened the kiss simultaneously, reaching the point where they needed more at the same time, moving in perfect sync. She dropped her head back and opened her mouth further. Less than a heartbeat later, his tongue pushed through her parted lips and into her mouth, unerringly finding her own. Within moments their tongues were moving together, sliding against each other, tangling, dancing. It felt like a brief taste of what it might be like if their entire bodies were pressed together, hard and yearning, sliding over each other, matching each other stroke for stroke. They moved faster, building momentum, picking up speed. More and more it seemed as though she couldn't breathe, trying to catch a breath whenever she could, not caring, needing more, of this, of him, of his mouth, of his taste.

She raised her hands to his chest, not even realizing she was doing it until she had, until she felt him there. Instinct made her smooth her hands over his front, to steady herself amidst the sensations rocking through her, to touch him, to feel him. A frustrated groan rose within her as her skin came into contact with the rough fabric of his coat. Beneath it she could feel him tense, feel the hard strength of his body, the firm muscles of his chest. But the coat and all the clothes in between kept her from feeling the heat of his skin, from touching him. She had to make do with his tongue working against hers, eagerly, hungrily. And it was good. It was so very good. But it wasn't enough. She wanted more. So much more.

The kiss must have been over long before she realized it, the sensations washing over her so overwhelming they remained well after the contact was broken. She finally opened her eyes to find him peering down at her. She realized with some amazement that her hands were on his shoulders now, gripping them tightly. She hadn't even realized she'd done it, she thought faintly, even as she absorbed how solid and rock-hard those shoulders felt. She didn't let go, still needing that strength, still feeling strangely boneless. The rough, ragged sounds of his breathing filled her ears. Or was it her own? Or both?

She stared into his eyes as they scanned her face, trying to read what she saw there. Heat. Desire, certainly. But also a sense of wonder, surprise even. She recognized it immediately, because she felt it, too. He hadn't expected everything they'd just experienced, what they'd felt in a mere kiss. Even as it registered, his eyes softened, shining with a tenderness that threatened to make her melt all over again.

He finally spoke, quietly, his voice deep and rough. "I really didn't want to like you."

Which meant that he did, of course. The kiss was confirmation enough of that. But hearing the sentiment spoken aloud, however indirectly, somehow made all the difference in the world as a fresh warmth spilled through her.

She smiled. "I could say I'm sorry, but I'm not."

"I can't say I am, either." One corner of his mouth quirked, and her heart lurched in response.

With a sigh, he suddenly released her entirely and stepped back, forcing her to slide her hands from his shoulders. "I should go," he said again.

Should you? she almost asked, even as part of her realized it was probably for the best. She wasn't sure what might happen next. This was already happening far faster than she'd ever let herself get carried away before.

"All right," she murmured.

His eyes stroked over her face. "Good night," he finally said, his voice thick.

"Good night," she echoed.

With one last searching glance, he ducked his head and turned back into the night.

Once again, she shut the door and leaned back against it. This time a sigh of pleasure worked its way from her lungs. She smiled as the memory of his lips against hers, his scent, his touch, washed over her. She'd never been kissed like that, with a combination of aching tenderness and raw hunger. It was hard to believe she'd reached the age of thirty-five without experiencing such a kiss. Or maybe such a thing was so rare she was lucky to have experienced it at all, the elusive combination of the right man and the right moment that some were never able to find.

One day, that voice in the back of her head echoed. *You've known him one day.*

Yet somehow it didn't matter. From the very first moment she'd met him and felt that sudden, inexplicable attraction, nothing she'd experienced with this man had been like anything she'd experienced before. How much she liked him. The sense of connection between them. Maybe it was only fitting that the physical aspect should unfold differently than she was used to as well. She certainly didn't regret it.

Her smile deepened, not just from the memory, but from the anticipation.

Because if this was the beginning—and she knew it was—she could hardly wait to see what happened next.

ARRIVING BACK AT HIS VEHICLE, Marcus threw himself into the driver's seat and just sat there for a few moments. He sucked in a ragged breath, trying to settle his pounding heart and the adrenaline rushing through him. Not to mention the aching hardness in his groin that was nowhere close to easing despite the freezing temperatures that should have been as effective as a cold shower.

He almost hadn't been able to stop it. As soon as he'd felt her hands on his chest, he'd almost responded, almost pushed her back up against the door and taken things a lot further right then and there. Only at the last possible moment had he remembered, and it had taken more strength than he'd known he had to break off the kiss. The knowledge had been welcome, necessary. No matter how badly he'd wanted it, and she'd seemed to too, it couldn't happen now. Not tonight. Probably not ever, but definitely not tonight.

He shook his head. He didn't know what it was about this woman that made him respond like a man who'd never been with a woman. Hell, even as a teenager he'd had more control than this. In spite of all the reasons he knew he shouldn't feel this way about her, he did. He couldn't deny it. He could only try to resist it.

With a sigh, he started the engine and shifted the car into gear. He'd ended the kiss for at least one very specific reason. He had things to take care of before it got too late.

Two hours later he pulled back onto her street. He stopped before reaching her house, parking in a space just down from it on the other side of the street. The position gave him a clear view of the front of the house without being too obvious about it. Perfect.

Shutting off the engine again, he settled back in his seat. It was going to be a long night.

If anything happened, if anything came close to happening, he would be here. If she tried calling him, if she needed help, he was right outside her door.

He could have offered to stay the night. It had been on the tip of his tongue when she'd said she intended to stay in the house. Common sense had killed the words before they came out, thank God. Given what had happened, he could only imagine what might have if they'd been alone together in her house.

Images burst into his head, along with remembered sensations. Swallowing hard, he blinked them away. Oh, yes. He could imagine.

Or maybe nothing would have happened. Maybe they both would have been able to show some restraint. Either way he would have been too distracted, thinking about her rather than staying aware of any possible threats, defeating the purpose of staying there at all. That left only one option, because he wasn't leaving her completely unprotected.

He suspected if he'd told her what he had in mind, she would have objected. She probably wouldn't have thought it was necessary and wouldn't have liked the idea of him sitting in the cold all night on her behalf. And once she figured out she wasn't going to change his mind, she might have insisted on him staying in the house, and he already knew that wasn't an option.

It was better this way. It didn't matter that she knew. It only mattered that he did.

Nothing was going to happen to her.

Not on his watch.

Chapter Nine

For the second time in a row, Regina spent a restless night. This time it wasn't the horrific images of murder that plagued her dreams. It was the face of a man, leaning close enough that she could read the emotion in his eyes, the smoky attraction burning in their dark depths. Even as she recognized it she felt it, smoldering inside her, the sensation as fierce in her dreams as it had been in reality.

The feeling remained long after she woke up. It wasn't until she booted her computer and opened the e-mail she found waiting for her in her inbox that she found a distraction. Lynn had come through for her, exactly as she'd expected. Every other thought vanished as she took in the words on the screen, her excitement building with each one. She'd barely finished reading when she dug out Waters's business card and reached for the phone.

He answered on the third ring. "Waters."

The sound of his voice on that single word was still enough to send a rush through her. In her haste, she hadn't thought about what she would say. She swallowed. "Marcus, it's Regina Garrett."

There was a long pause before he finally said, "Yes, Regina."

The cautious note in his voice broke through her excitement. She immediately recognized what caused it, the memory of last night's encounter rushing back to mind once more. She hadn't even thought about any potential awkwardness between them the next day, her thoughts so consumed by the experience itself. "I hope I'm not bothering you too early," she said slowly.

"Not at all. Everything okay?"

"Fine. I just received some new information on the case. I had my investigator do a background check on this Troy Lewis that Eric Howard told us about. It turns out he has an extensive criminal record, including—get this—burglary."

She wasn't entirely sure what reaction she'd expected, but the silence that greeted her statement wasn't it. Finally, when she was about to speak again, he said, "Yes, I know."

"You do?"

"I did a background check myself."

Of course he had, she thought with a touch of embarrassment. He was a police detective. In her overblown excitement, she'd forgotten exactly who she was talking to. In fact, she realized, with his resources, he'd probably received the results faster than she had. And if he'd called in and requested them yesterday after he dropped her off… His reserve suddenly took on a new meaning.

"When did you find out?"

She heard him exhale softly. "Yesterday afternoon."

"So you knew this last night."

"Some of it."

"Were you even planning on telling me?"

His hesitation before answering told her all she needed to know. "I hadn't decided yet."

"But you were leaning toward 'no.'"

"After what happened in your office, not to mention everything else, I'm not sure your continued involvement in the case is a good idea."

"My involvement in the case has already been accomplished. There's no taking it back now. I didn't ask for any of this. I didn't do anything to provoke this person to leave a tongue on my porch, and the simple act of walking into my office got me attacked. As long as this person is going to pull this garbage, I'm not going to sit by and wait to see what they try to do to me next."

"Maybe you should leave town, take that trip you had planned."

"I already lost the reservation, and I'm not running away. If you think I'm the kind of person who would, I have to seriously doubt your powers of observation."

"Thinking it and hoping for it are two different things," he sighed. "I just don't want you to get hurt."

Something in the sudden softness of his voice brought back last night's close encounter, the tenderness she'd seen in his eyes. A light shudder trembled along her nerve endings, and she reminded herself he wasn't saying this to be controlling or condescending. She believed he really did care, and the knowledge took some of the anger out of her response.

"The best way to ensure that doesn't happen is to catch this person," she said. "Let me help you do that."

"Do you mean you can help me, or you're willing to let *me* help *you?*" he asked, a hint of humor in his words.

"There doesn't have to be a difference. All that matters is catching this person."

"Before they try something again."

"That would be my preference."

"Mine, too." He paused. "I guess there's no way I can talk you into not trying to talk to this guy yourself."

"None at all."

"Fine. Pick you up in thirty?"

Anticipation shot through her. "I'll be ready."

As promised, when Marcus pulled into her driveway a half hour later, the door immediately opened and Regina stepped outside. He kept the motor running and watched her approach.

Once again, he was struck by how beautiful she was. It seemed like he should be used to it by now, not almost caught off-guard by it every time he saw her. Yet every time, it was like a fresh blow to his gut, sending his adrenaline surging. Even now, he couldn't take his eyes off her, tracking every movement as she came down the steps and walked down the path toward him. Kissing her hadn't diminished what he'd been feeling for her one bit. Now that he'd tasted her, now that he'd felt her soft, warm body pressed against his, he just wanted more.

Almost as much as he wanted her out of this. He hadn't expected her to give in willingly, knew she would insist on seeing the case through to the end. He wanted to be angry with her for it, but he couldn't. It was who she was, and damned if he didn't like who she was.

He'd finally left around five-thirty that morning when it seemed unlikely anything was going to happen. After catching a few hours of sleep, he'd made his way to the station. He'd used his time last night to make some calls and ask around about her, needing more than ever to know that his attraction to this woman wasn't overriding his instincts. It had taken a while, but he'd finally gotten some people, cops he respected, to admit, however grudgingly, that when it came to defense attorneys, Regina Garrett was one of the good ones. She was good at her job, she was ethical, and if she made them look bad more often than any of them would have liked, well, that said as much about them as it did about her.

It was what he'd wanted to hear—and it wasn't. Because it didn't change who she was, what she did, not really. It just meant his instincts weren't wrong, leaving him fewer reasons to resist a woman he knew he had no business being with.

She arrived at the car and pulled the passenger door open, sliding in beside him. "Good morning," she said with a smile.

"Morning."

Her eyes tracked over his face, almost hungrily it seemed. Her smile deepened the slightest fraction before she turned and reached for her seat belt. "Should we go?"

"Sure," he said. Shifting the car into gear, he started to back out of the driveway.

He waited for her to say something about what had happened between them last night. She didn't. Neither did he. Nobody had to. He still felt the knowledge pounding through his body, saw it in her eyes.

"I'm assuming you already received the background check on Adrian Moore," she said instead.

He nodded. "He's former military. Not somebody I would expect to be working as a rich man's driver, but evidently he and Cole Madison grew up together. I guess Madison really moved up in the world and decided to help out an old friend with a job."

"So Moore is both a trained fighter and has reason to be loyal. Not a bad person to have on the payroll if you want to have somebody threatened."

"Which leads us back to why Madison might have wanted him to threaten the Deckers."

"Hopefully Troy Lewis can provide some insight."

Lewis's last known address was a house not far from Lauren Decker's home, probably not surprising given that they'd dated. As they pulled on to the street, Marcus saw his original intention of keeping Regina away from the man had been a good one. She had no business being in this neighborhood on her own. He wasn't sure she should be here at all, even with him. As long as she was, he was going to keep her close to his side.

Spotting the house, they parked across the street and climbed out of the car. Despite the cold, there was a man sitting on the front step, a lit cigarette dangling between his fingers. As they approached, he raised the cigarette to his lips and inhaled deeply, letting a long cloud of smoke curl from his mouth.

"Troy Lewis?" Marcus asked, more as a greeting than as a real question. He'd seen Lewis's photo from his most recent arrest, and there was little question that this was him.

"Who's asking?" the man asked with all the belligerence Marcus would have expected.

"Detective Waters, Chicago PD."

"Detective," Lewis echoed with a sneer. "Fancy."

"I'd like to ask you a few questions about Jeremy Decker."

Lewis snorted. "I heard he got himself killed. Too bad for him."

"And for his sister. I hear the two of you dated for a while."

The man's eyes narrowed with suspicion. "Yeah, so?"

"You don't sound too broken up about his death."

"I'm not. I couldn't care less. The guy acted like he was better than everybody else. He was always talking trash about me, always telling her I wasn't good enough for her. She ended up dropping me, said she deserved a 'higher class of man.' I wonder who put that idea in her head?"

Marcus was surprised the man would admit to being dumped until Lewis smirked. "I hear she's all on her own now and stuck with a kid. Looks like that didn't turn out so good for her, did it? Guess Mr. Higher Class figured out she wasn't so great, either."

Of course. He would admit it as long as Lauren came out looking worse in his story.

"So you're not the father of Lauren's baby?" Regina asked.

The man held up his hands, eyes going wide. "Hell, no. I haven't seen her since last year. No way that kid is mine."

Marcus figured they'd gotten far enough off-track. "I'm sure you heard Jeremy Decker was arrested for a burglary several months ago."

Lewis grinned. "Yep. Guess he wasn't so perfect after all."

"You wouldn't happen to know anything about that burglary, would you?"

"Nope."

"You've had some experience with burglary yourself though, haven't you?"

"That's what the cops said. Doesn't make it true."

"And you're sure you don't know anything about the burglary Jeremy Decker was accused of committing?"

"How many times do you want me to say it? I don't know anything about it."

"All right." Time to try a different tack. Marcus leaned in. "The thing is, as far as we can tell, Decker had no criminal experience. Did he ever give you the impression he might be interested in a little breaking and entering? Maybe he was a little too interested in what you might know since he thought you had some experience?"

Lewis snickered. "No, *he* never was."

Marcus narrowed his eyes, wondering if he'd heard the man right. "So 'he' wasn't. But someone was?"

Lewis briefly looked startled as if he realized he'd said too much before he gave his head a vigorous shake. "Nah, man. Nothing like that. I told you. I don't know anything."

Interesting. "One last question. Where were you Tuesday night?"

"Watching the game at Smokey's Bar down the block. Half the neighborhood was there. You shouldn't have any problem finding people to tell you I was, too."

Based on Lewis's smugness, Marcus didn't doubt he was right. He wondered whether it was because it was true or because Lewis knew plenty of people would be willing to lie for him. Marcus had a feeling it was the former, which left them back where they'd started.

"All right, Mr. Lewis. Thank you for your time," he made himself say.

Neither he nor Regina spoke until they were back in the car. "I don't know about you, but that wasn't what I was expecting," she said. "Did you get the same impression that I did?"

"That someone was interested in Lewis's

criminal exploits, but it wasn't Jeremy Decker. Lauren?"

"Eric Howard did say she had a wild side. It could be one of the reasons she was drawn to Lewis's bad boy thing."

"At least until she dumped him," he pointed out.

"Normally I'd think a guy like that was lying to get out of responsibility for his child, but I don't think he was. He was too self-satisfied. So who is the father of Lauren's baby? Or does it even matter?"

"Either way, I'm thinking we may need to learn more about Lauren Decker to see if she has more of a role in this than it seemed."

"Not a problem." Regina pulled out her cell phone. "I had my investigator do a check on her as well. She sent me a message early this morning, but I was so focused on the Lewis and Moore information I didn't really get a chance to read through it. Oh—and it looks like she just sent me something else a little while ago."

Marcus watched her reaction as she thumbed through her messages, focusing on the screen of her device. It wasn't long before she was frowning, two little lines appearing between her eyebrows. Somehow even that didn't diminish her beauty.

"What is it?" he asked when she didn't say anything.

"I asked Lynn—that's my investigator—to look for any connections between Jeremy and the Madisons. And she found one—between Lauren and the Madisons."

He frowned, his expression matching hers. "Lauren?"

Regina finally looked up at him. "It seems she's mostly worked as a waitress over the years, starting when she was sixteen and working her way up to more upscale restaurants. Last fall she had a job at Parsons Steakhouse downtown. She wasn't there long, a couple months from the sound of it. The restaurant is just down the street from the offices of Gaines Financial."

It didn't take long for the implications to settle in. "Parsons. That's the restaurant Tracy Madison mentioned her husband liked to go a lot. That can't be a coincidence."

"I don't think so either," she agreed. "If he does like to go there that often, they could have met. Lynn didn't have a chance to go there herself yet and see if anyone there remembers Cole and Lauren meeting or talking to each other, but she wanted to let me know."

"Tell her not to bother." Marcus shoved

his key in the ignition and started the engine. "We'll do it ourselves. You have the address?"

"Yep." She rattled it off even as he started to pull away from the curb.

"Are you thinking what I'm thinking?" he asked.

"I bet I am," she said, a smile in her voice as she typed into her phone. "But why don't you tell me what you're thinking?"

"So we know Lauren was looking for a 'higher class of man.' If she met Madison, a rich, handsome older man like him would fit the bill."

"Never mind that he was already married. Maybe she knew it, maybe she didn't. A man like that would only be looking for a good time. I can't imagine he would have reacted well when she got pregnant."

"Especially when she decided to keep the baby," Marcus said. "He might have dropped her, maybe tried to pay her off."

"And then *she* might not have reacted well. She might have acted out, might have tried to get even."

"Like breaking into his house and stealing some of his wife's jewelry?" Marcus finished the thought.

They exchanged a glance, clearly very

much on the same page. Regina shook her head in amazement. "We've been looking at this all wrong. I knew there was more to the burglary than Jeremy being guilty of it. I even thought about who he might have been covering for since he wasn't being forthcoming. A sibling was a logical choice, but Lauren had no criminal record and at the time there was no reason to believe she had a motive. Plus, she was four months pregnant. Except that probably *was* her motive."

"If Decker suspected what she was going to do for some reason, he might have gone to stop her."

"He could have touched the window without thinking, especially if he found it broken and had to go into the house to get her out of there. And when the police arrived, he wouldn't have wanted his pregnant sister to be arrested, so he let himself be captured, providing the diversion to let her get away."

"So Lauren wasn't arrested, but was left alone to fend for herself," he deduced.

"Jeremy said she left the city to stay with relatives when she had the baby. She just came back this month."

"Because he was getting out of jail?"

"No, she had already been back for a few weeks by then. Jeremy told me, said it was perfect timing when I gave him the news of his release."

"It couldn't have been easy for her, a young woman with an infant, trying to take care of it all by herself. Hard to stay away when you have a house here you own so you don't have to worry about paying for an apartment. Not to mention she probably could have used some financial help."

"And naturally she would have contacted the baby's father," Regina said. "Especially since he has plenty of money."

"She's young and desperate. She might have been willing to take whatever he'd offer."

"While her older brother, who'd been protecting her all her life and had just gotten out of jail, might not have been satisfied with what the man had to offer or the way he was treating his sister. Do you think that's why Jeremy wanted to speak with me? Maybe he wanted legal advice, especially if they were being threatened."

"And they might have decided to shut him up rather than let anyone else find out. A love child might be a secret worth killing over if you're a married man working for your father-in-law."

They both fell silent, the implications laying heavily in the air.

"If this all turns out to be true, then you were right," Marcus said. "Decker was innocent."

"Good to know I can still count on my instincts," Regina said. "But all we have is a theory. We still have to prove it."

"Then let's do it," he said firmly, anticipation stirring in his gut. "We'll start with the restaurant."

Chapter Ten

Parsons was exactly what Regina would have expected for an upscale steakhouse. The walls were wood-paneled, the furnishings high-class and masculine, the lighting low-key, with each of the tables and booths lit in a way that seemed to isolate it from those around it. Given its location, Regina could imagine rich and powerful men gathering here to conduct business deals while smoking cigars and eating red meat. Only the cigars seemed to be missing, the one allowance to changing times. Otherwise, the restaurant fit the image to a T.

It was still early. Whatever passed for a lunch rush likely hadn't yet started. A hostess looked up as they walked through the door. "Good afternoon. Welcome to Parsons."

"Good afternoon," Marcus said smoothly. "You know, I've never been here before, but I've heard good things about it. A friend of mine recommended it. I'm not sure if you know him. Cole Madison?"

The woman nodded with a smile. "Why, yes. We see Mr. Madison at least once a week. I'm happy to hear he's pleased enough with our establishment to recommend it."

"So am I," Marcus agreed. "Madison's a… *friendly* man, wouldn't you say?"

The smile never wavered, but Regina saw a hint of wariness enter the woman's expression. "I'm not sure what you mean."

"It doesn't matter," Marcus said amiably. He produced his badge and identified himself, causing the hostess's smile to finally die. "Is there a manager we could speak with, someone who'd be familiar with former employees?"

"Of course. Let me get him for you." Turning on her heel, she hurried away down a hall to the right.

"Very clever," Regina mused under her breath. "If you asked outright, they might not have admitted Madison came here, not wanting to risk offending a regular."

"I had a feeling this was the kind of place willing to keep its regulars' secrets," Marcus agreed.

"Like the secret about him being overly friendly with the service staff? I have a feeling she knew exactly what you were talking about."

"So do I."

The sound of footsteps approaching cut off anything else they might have said. A balding man with thin-rimmed glasses emerged from the hallway, the hostess trailing behind. His expression was studiously polite as he greeted them. "I'm Glen Cowan, the manager here. I'm told you had some questions about a former employee?"

"That's right," Marcus said. "Is there somewhere we can talk?"

"Of course. My office is right this way." He gestured toward the hall he'd appeared from, leaving them to follow him.

They stepped into a small office, Cowan moving behind the desk and motioning toward the chairs on the other side. "What exactly is this about?"

"A young woman named Lauren Decker," Marcus said. "I was told she worked here last year."

"Yes, I remember her, although I admit I'd almost forgotten all about her until you said her name. She didn't last long. Maybe a month or two."

"Can you tell me what happened? Was she terminated?"

"No, she quit. As I recall, she didn't even give notice. Said she didn't need the job anymore."

"After only a couple of months?" Marcus said.

Cowan shrugged. "Who knows? Maybe she won the lottery."

Yes, Regina mused, maybe she thought she had, in a way.

"Was she a good employee?" Marcus asked.

The man hesitated, tellingly, Regina thought. "I don't remember any problems with her job performance," he said carefully. "She was very…outgoing, very friendly with the customers. They seemed to like her."

She was a flirt, Regina read between the lines. She met Marcus's eyes. From the knowing gleam in them, he'd made the same interpretation.

"Is there anything else you can tell us about her employment here?" Marcus asked.

"No," Cowan said, his casualness forced. "I can't think of anything. Like I said, she wasn't here very long. I barely remember her."

That was funny. Regina thought he seemed to remember Lauren quite well.

"All right then," Marcus said. Thank you, Mr. Cowan. I appreciate your time."

Two minutes later, he and Regina stood outside the restaurant. "What do you think?" he asked.

"If Cole and Lauren did begin an affair, it would have been awkward to have her still working at his favorite restaurant, serving him at least once a week. It would explain why she quit."

"And she wouldn't have done it without some assurance the relationship was worth quitting for, maybe even that he'd take care of her."

"So it was serious, at least for her," Regina said. "Where do you want to go now?"

Marcus turned and glanced down the street in the direction of the Gaines Financial offices. "As long as we're in the neighborhood, we might as well pay Madison a visit. Yesterday I asked him if he knew Jeremy. I'm thinking I asked him about the wrong Decker. Maybe it's time to fix that."

As he had the day before, Cole Madison was willing to see them, this time sending his assistant out to escort them back to his office. He greeted them with the same forced heartiness, which Marcus recognized as an obvious attempt to seem cooperative in an effort to divert suspicion. This time, though, there was a hint of apology in his expression as they stepped into his office and he rose to meet them.

"Detectives, I'm afraid I haven't yet had a chance to request the information you asked for."

The identity of the person who'd paid Lauren Decker a visit yesterday, Marcus recalled. Not that he'd expected Madison to put any particular rush on providing that information. He couldn't wait to see how the man reacted to the news they already knew. "That's all right," he said. "Our investigation has actually shifted focus since yesterday and I'd like to ask you about something else."

"I see," Madison said warily, his tone suggesting otherwise. "What is it?"

"Yesterday you said you didn't know Jeremy Decker."

"That's right."

"What about his sister, Lauren?"

The man didn't say anything for a long moment, simply staring at him. "What about her?"

"So you do know her?"

"No, I don't believe so."

"That's interesting, because she used to work at a restaurant down the street from this building. Parsons Steakhouse? I believe your wife said it's your favorite."

"What's your point?"

"You're sure you didn't know her? It sounds like you're in there all the time."

"That's true, but I'm afraid I couldn't tell you the names of any of the people who work there."

"Sure, I understand," Marcus said. "It's a strange coincidence that the brother of someone who worked at your favorite restaurant would be arrested for breaking into your home, isn't it?"

"Unquestionably."

"Can you think of any reason why Lauren Decker's brother would want to break into your home?"

"Not at all."

"Can you think of any reason why he would even be in your neighborhood?"

"I didn't know the man, so I can't explain any of his actions."

"But you did know Lauren Decker."

The man hesitated briefly, no more than a split second, but enough for Marcus to notice the telltale sign of someone who wondered if he'd slipped up before catching himself. "No, I told you I didn't."

"That's right, you did," Marcus said agreeably. "However, if you did know her, had an affair with her and broke up with her, she might have decided to lash out in some way, like breaking into the home you share with your wife."

"That's an interesting story, Detective, but one which has no basis in reality."

"She especially might have lashed out if she was dumped by her lover while she was pregnant, wouldn't she?"

"I couldn't say."

"Lauren Decker has an infant daughter, did you know that?"

The man smiled, a pale imitation of the broad one he'd displayed earlier, thin-lipped with no teeth. "How could I?"

"Of course," Marcus said wryly. "Because you didn't know her."

"That's right."

"So it's not possible that you had an affair with her and you are the father of her child?"

"Of course not." The man laughed, even his bluster sounding fake.

"And that's why you had one of your employees visit her yesterday, perhaps in an attempt to pay her off or threaten her into leaving town with your child?"

"That's absurd."

"Really? Because as we were leaving the building yesterday, we saw the man who visited Lauren Decker. He was in a car parked in front of the building. It turns out he's your personal driver, Adrian Moore."

As Marcus had expected, Madison hadn't seen that piece of information coming at all. He froze again, his entire expression going slack for a brief moment before he managed to regain himself. "That's news to me, Detective."

"You're saying you didn't send Mr. Moore to talk to Lauren Decker?"

"I had no reason to."

"So it's just another coincidence that your driver was at the home of a woman who worked at your favorite restaurant, whose brother was arrested for breaking into your house."

"I can't explain it," Madison said with a forced chuckle.

"Of course," Marcus repeated slowly. "Because you *don't* know Lauren Decker."

"No," Madison said. "I don't."

Marcus stripped every trace of false humor from his voice and pinned the man with his stare. "Then I guess it's not worth mentioning that if anything should happen to Lauren

Decker or her child, the person responsible will answer for it. I personally guarantee it."

Madison held his gaze, though it was clear to Marcus that it took some effort. "You're right. It's not worth mentioning, and in no way relevant to me."

"Because you don't know her," Marcus said one last time, unable to keep a slightly mocking edge from the statement. "Then I'm sorry to have taken up your time. It should be easy enough to find out who the father of Lauren Decker's child is. If it's not you," he added after a beat.

"It's not," Madison said.

"So you said," Marcus replied easily. "Thank you for seeing us. We'll see ourselves out." He turned to find Regina had already taken his cue and started toward the door. They quickly exited Madison's office. Marcus felt the man's eyes on them the whole way.

They didn't speak until they were alone in the elevator heading back down to the lobby.

"That was interesting," Regina said mildly. "Why didn't you confront him more directly?"

"I didn't think it would do any good. Do you really think he was going to admit it?"

"No, although I didn't believe him for a second when he said he didn't know her."

"Neither did I. I'm more positive than ever that he is the father of Lauren's child."

"So why not say it point-blank? Why the cat-and-mouse routine?"

"If he is having Lauren Decker threatened in some way, I wanted to send a message that he needs to back off. Right now, ensuring that nothing happens to her and we don't end up with another murder victim before we can prove Madison is responsible is a top priority."

"Do you really think it'll work?"

"Maybe not," he admitted. "But it was worth a try."

"So what now?"

"Obviously I wasn't entirely truthful with Madison. It won't be easy to prove who the father of Lauren's child is. The only person who can confirm that is Lauren herself."

"We need her to finally tell us the truth," Regina concluded. "It's not going to be easy, especially if she's already scared."

"Then we just have to convince her that there are worse things to be scared of than telling us the truth."

THIS TIME THERE WERE no signs of any visitors when they arrived at Lauren's house. The single car parked in the driveway was the only vehicle in view.

The sight struck Regina as sad, emphasizing just how alone Lauren Decker was. The young woman really shouldn't be on her own during such a difficult time. Regina wished Lauren had called her, even though she hadn't really expected her to. Now that she suspected she knew the nature of the secrets Lauren was keeping, Regina could better understand why the young woman had cut herself off from others. She'd already lost her brother because of this; she wouldn't want to risk losing anyone else. Hopefully they could somehow convince her she didn't have to be alone in this.

When they arrived at the door, Regina knocked gently, not wanting to disturb the baby if she was napping again. A full minute passed without a response. She rapped a little louder, still not wanting to go too far. They were going to have a hard enough time getting the woman to confide in them. Waking her sleeping infant wasn't likely to do much to get them on her good side.

Just when Regina was considering knocking a third time and even louder, the door slowly opened. Lauren scowled at them. "More questions?"

"A few," Regina said, offering an apologetic smile. "May we come in?"

Lauren sighed and opened the door fully. "Sure."

They stepped into the living room. Regina was surprised to see some empty boxes spread out around the room, as well as a few that already had some items in them. Several rolls of packaging tape and bubble wrap lay on the coffee table.

"Are you packing?" Marcus asked.

Lauren moved to a nearby shelf and began pulling the books from it, placing them in a nearby box, her motions sharp and agitated. "I'm leaving town. There's nothing left for me here. I never should have come back in the first place."

"Are you leaving after the funeral?" Regina asked.

"There's not going to be one. I'm having Jeremy cremated. Now that I know what was done to him, I wouldn't be able to take looking at the body."

It made a certain amount of sense, but there was little to no emotion in the woman's words. Her face remained blank, her movements robotic, as though she was just going through the motions.

"Well, about what happened to Jeremy,"

Marcus said. "We want to ask you about Cole Madison."

Regina was watching closely to see how Lauren reacted to the name. As far as she could tell, the young woman didn't react at all. After a moment she simply asked, "Who's that?"

"He's the man whose house Jeremy was accused of breaking into."

"What about him?"

"He's also a regular customer at the restaurant downtown where you used to work."

Lauren stared at him blankly. "So?"

"Are you saying you don't know him?"

"That's right."

"Isn't it a strange coincidence that your brother was arrested for breaking into the house of someone who eats at least once a week at the restaurant where you used to work?"

"I guess it is."

"We spoke to the manager there. He said you quit without giving any notice."

She shrugged. "I didn't like the job."

"Where have you worked since then?"

For the first time, Lauren seemed at a loss for words, the pause lasting slightly too long. "I haven't been able to find a job. Things have been crazy with the baby and everything."

"But you wouldn't have been pregnant when you quit. You didn't have something else lined up before quitting without giving any notice?"

"No," Lauren said. "I just didn't want to work there anymore."

Regina shot Marcus a glance, once again appreciating his patience. He remained cool and calm, asking the questions in a non-confrontational tone, showing no frustration or anger at her evasions. "All right," he said. "Let me ask you another question. Who is your baby's father?"

"An old boyfriend," Lauren said automatically. "He's not a part of my life anymore."

"You mean Troy Lewis?"

Her eyes flared briefly. "How do you know about him?"

"We spoke with him this morning. He said he's not the baby's father."

"He's a liar. You can't believe a word he says."

"He says you broke up last year, long before you would have become pregnant."

"I just told you, he's a liar."

"He says you dropped him for somebody else, somebody with more money."

"I don't know how many times I have to say it. He's a liar."

"I don't believe he would lie about that. Admitting that you dumped him doesn't make him look too good."

"I can't explain how his mind works. I never could."

"So you didn't break up with him?"

"Yes," Lauren said. "But only after."

"Who did you break up with him for?"

"Nobody. I was just sick of his garbage."

"It wasn't for Cole Madison?"

"No."

"And Cole Madison isn't your baby's father?"

"No."

Regina had to hand it to her. The young woman wasn't giving an inch. Under different circumstances, Regina might have been willing to take that as an indication she should believe her. But given the fact that she'd already lied to them in the past, Regina remained highly skeptical.

"Lauren, are you in danger?" she asked gently. "Is that the real reason you've suddenly decided to leave town? Is that the reason you left the city to have your baby in the first place?"

"I don't know what you're talking about."

"If Madison is threatening you, we can help you—"

"The way you helped Jeremy?

Regina almost flinched. The woman's words were flat, her expression blank, but they stung just the same. Even worse, Regina couldn't entirely dispute them, a pang of guilt hitting home. "I wish I could have helped Jeremy," she admitted softly. "I wish I'd had some idea of what he was facing. If I had, I would have done everything possible to help him, but I didn't know. He didn't get a chance to tell me. That's why I need to know what you're facing. It's the only way I can help, and if you'll let me, I promise I will do everything I can."

Lauren simply shook her head and looked away. "I don't need your help. I'll be fine on my own. Now, is that it? I have a lot of packing to do."

Regina glanced at Marcus, but he didn't appear to have any better idea of what to say than she did. Lauren seemed to have made up her mind, and the trouble was, Regina couldn't entirely blame her.

"That's all for now," Marcus said. "We'll let you get back to your packing."

A minute later, they stood outside, the closed door behind them.

"So where do we go from here?" Regina sighed as they made their way back to the car.

"I don't know. We can't prove Madison is

the baby's father, and without that there's no reason to believe he's the one who's after her or the one who had Jeremy killed. No judge is going to order a DNA test. We could track down the birth certificate, but considering what we think Madison is capable of, I have to believe Lauren is smart enough not to have listed him, especially after having to leave town to give birth in the first place."

"I agree. She has to know what kind of man he is by now. Based on what we saw yesterday and Lauren's plan to make a quick exit, he's still threatening her. But again, as long as she's not willing to confide in us, there's no way to prove any of it."

"We could try to lean on Moore, except with his background and history with Madison, I don't think he'll give up anything. We don't even have any proof that he's threatening Lauren or done anything illegal to use as leverage."

"So what does that leave us with?" she asked, her frustration growing. It felt as though they were so close. She was convinced they had the answers they needed. But those answers wouldn't do them any good without the evidence to back them up, and when it came to proof, they seemed to have hit a dead end.

They reached the car. When they were

both inside, Regina expected him to start the engine. Instead, he just sat there in the driver's seat, staring straight ahead, apparently deep in thought.

Finally he said, "Tracy Madison."

After a beat, Regina nodded slowly, understanding. "You want to use her against her husband."

"She's the person Madison would want to keep this from the most. Do you think she'd believe this was all a coincidence?"

"No," Regina agreed. "I don't. So it might be interesting to see how she'll react to the news."

Before he could respond, his cell phone suddenly buzzed. He pulled it out and checked the screen. Whatever he saw couldn't have been good, because he grimaced and said, "Excuse me for a second," before answering.

Curious, Regina watched him take the call. He mostly listened, uttering only a few terse comments. Finally he disconnected the call, an even more troubled expression on his face.

"Everything okay?" she asked carefully.

"I doubt it. My captain wants to see me immediately."

"What about?"

His lips thinned. "This case."

A whisper of unease slid through her. "Did he say why?"

"No, but it didn't sound good." Shaking his head, he started the engine. "I'll drop you back at your house on the way."

It was on the tip of her tongue to offer to come with him. She managed to hold back the words. She had no business being there, no matter how much she wanted to offer her support.

Because based on the look on his face, he was going to need it. She didn't know why his captain would want to see him right away regarding this case, but something told her it was going to be trouble.

Chapter Eleven

"Where are you on the Decker investigation?"

Captain Keith Dunn didn't waste any time, throwing the question at Marcus the second he closed the door to the captain's office behind him.

Marcus turned to face the man. "I think I'm pretty close. I have a good idea who's responsible. I'm just trying to prove it."

Dunn scowled at him. "By harassing Cole Madison and his family?"

Marcus frowned, caught by surprise. "I haven't been harassing them. Madison has come up several times over the course of the investigation, so I naturally went to interview him."

"That's not what I've been hearing, or more important, what some of the higher-ups have been hearing. I got a call a little while ago telling me to rein you in before you go pissing off any more people."

"I didn't know Madison had that much political clout."

"He doesn't, but his father-in-law does, and he's screaming harassment to some people who are now breathing down my neck. Now, what exactly do you have?"

Marcus briefly explained everything they'd learned so far. "Based on what we know, I think Madison is behind the murder of Jeremy Decker and may be threatening his sister to keep the fact that he fathered her baby from coming out."

"That's right—you *think*. You have no evidence. You're just throwing around these theories with nothing to go on but speculation. And until you come up with some actual proof that Cole Madison is involved, he and his family are off-limits."

Marcus barely tamped down the anger that threatened to erupt. Losing his cool wasn't going to get him anywhere. "So that's it? Because he has connections, he's going to get away with it, and you're okay with that?"

"I'm not saying he's going to get away with it. I'm saying if he is guilty, then find some proof. It sounds like you could use a fresh angle. So far you've pissed these people off, but it hasn't produced anything concrete."

"And cutting off access to them isn't going to help me find something concrete."

"Regardless, you're going to have to find another way."

"And if there isn't one, then what? He just gets away with it?"

Dunn stared at him, his eyes narrowing. "You're taking this awfully personally."

"What can I say? I don't like people getting away with murder because they have connections."

"Interesting attitude coming from someone who's been spending a lot of time with a certain lady defense attorney."

Marcus stiffened. "I don't know what you mean."

"Don't give me that. I hear you adopted Regina Garrett as your de facto partner on this. In fact, I hear you've been passing her off as a detective."

"I never said she was a detective, and neither did she."

"But you knew that's what they thought, and you didn't bother to clear things up for them. What was she even doing there at all?"

"She's a valuable resource who knows the major players and has been able to provide some insight into the case and the people involved."

"I hear she's not bad to look at, either."

"It has nothing to do with that," Marcus said immediately.

"I also hear you've been asking around about her, too."

"Like I said, she's a resource. Seemed like a good idea to find out the kind of person I'm dealing with."

"Uh-huh," Dunn said, his skepticism clear. "In any case, leave the Madisons alone. Unless you can come up with something that's more than just guesswork, they're off-limits to you, got it?"

"Got it," Marcus made himself say as calmly as possible.

"Good." With a nod, Dunn lowered his attention to the papers on his desk, the dismissal clear.

Without another word, Marcus turned and stalked out of the office.

Polinsky was at his desk, a smug look on his face, his eyes shooting daggers as Marcus approached his own desk. In no mood for his attitude at the moment, Marcus had every intention of ignoring the man.

Unfortunately, Polinsky wasn't the type to be ignored. "I told you it was a mistake to let that woman anywhere near the investigation," he said as soon as Marcus was within earshot. "She's nothing but trouble."

"She's contributed a lot more to the case than you have," Marcus shot back.

"Hey, if she wants to put garbage back on the street, maybe she *should* be the one to clean up the mess when something happens to them. I've got plenty of cases where the people *didn't* deserve what happened to them. So do you."

Marcus stared at the man for a long moment before slowly shaking his head. "You know, Polinsky, I put up with a lot from you because I thought at least you were good at the job. But if that's how you feel, then you really don't have a clue."

Before Polinsky could say a word, Marcus turned and quickly made his way through the room. He had to get out of there. He had to think.

Evidently he had to figure out a new way to prove what he and Regina believed. And he would. Letting Madison get away with everything wasn't an option.

But using his wife to get to him had been a last-ditch approach anyway, a Hail Mary with no guarantee of success. With that no longer a possibility, Marcus had no idea how to prove any of it.

He had to come up with something.

But as his mind remained stubbornly blank, he started to wonder with a sinking heart if there was a chance in hell that he actually could.

REGINA HAD EXPECTED—and hoped, really— to hear from Marcus within a few hours after he dropped her off at her house, as soon as his meeting was over. But the afternoon passed without a word. After a while she had to force herself to stop glancing at the clock so often before she drove herself crazy.

Instead, she tried to focus on the investigation. Curled up on the couch with her laptop, her notes spread around her, she went over everything they'd learned, everything Lynn had sent her. Going through Tracy Madison might work, but if it didn't, they'd need more options. There had to be some way to prove what they suspected, something she'd missed, an answer she hadn't considered. Jeremy's killer couldn't get away with it. But no matter how hard she tried to come up with an answer, it failed to surface, leaving her with only more frustration.

It was well after seven when she heard a knock at her front door, the sound both a surprise and a relief. Anything to get her away from her notes was welcome at this point. Puzzled who it might be, she rose from the couch and checked through the window.

And there he was.

The foolish excitement that filled her quickly turned to concern once she opened the door and really saw him. He didn't look up when she opened the door. He stood with his hands buried in his pockets, his eyes downcast, his jaw clenched. Tension radiated from every inch of his body.

"Marcus?" she said carefully. "What's wrong?"

He opened his mouth to say something, then slammed it shut, shaking his head. "Can I come in?"

"Of course," she said. She moved out of the doorway, allowing him to slide past, then closed the door behind him.

He'd stopped a few feet into the living room, and just stood there. Something about the sight of him made her heart squeeze in her chest. He was such a massive presence filling the space, big and strong and undeniably male. Yet as he stood there, he made for an almost forlorn figure, seeming strangely lost. She could see that while he was here physically, his thoughts were far away, something weighing on him heavily.

When he didn't say anything, she finally asked, "How'd your meeting go?"

He exhaled sharply. "Not well. It seems Donald Gaines called in some favors with his high-powered connections and I've been told to back off from his family. Unless I come up with some concrete evidence that Cole Madison is involved in Jeremy Decker's death, the Madisons are officially off-limits."

Regina frowned. "That's interesting. If they didn't want to talk to you, all they had to do was hire an attorney to run interference. I'm sure these people already have an entire firm on retainer who would have made it impossible for you to get anywhere near their clients. Instead they chose a way that took more effort and looks a lot more suspicious."

"It's also cheaper and more effective," he pointed out.

"True. And if they went to that much trouble, at least you know you're getting to them."

"For all the good it does me."

"So what do we do now?"

He sighed heavily. "Hell if I know. I've been driving around all afternoon trying to figure out a new approach, some new angle to use, and I didn't come up with anything."

"Don't beat yourself up about it," she said.

"I've been doing the same thing and haven't had any better luck."

"So I don't know where that leaves us. Damn it. I'm actually starting to think Decker's killer is going to get away with it." He shook his head. "Are you going to say it?"

"Say what?"

"'I told you so.' It's like you said. Rich people get a different kind of justice."

"I wouldn't do that," she said softly. She hated that he would think so. She took no pleasure in seeing him so unhappy.

And yet, there was something about his reaction she found reassuring. His feelings weren't the result of being naive. He was old enough to know how the world unfortunately worked too much of the time, especially given his job and the things he had to see on a daily basis. And yet, he wasn't entirely hardened against it. That kind of injustice was still capable of bothering him, because he was a good man. He still cared enough about justice being served to be deeply frustrated when it wasn't. She knew what that was like, to fight so hard and care so deeply about something and sometimes still have there be nothing she could do. Knew what it was like to be eaten up by the wrongness of it. Eventually there was no choice but to move on. There were always new cases, new battles to be fought. She hoped the day never came when she would be so jaded and worn out that injustice didn't bother her and she simply accepted that that was how things worked. Clearly that day hadn't arrived for him, either. Somehow she suspected that for this man it never would. Partly because of his past experience, but mostly, she sensed, because he really was a good man.

Suddenly compelled to touch him, she reached out and placed her hand on his arm. "Don't worry. We'll figure it out."

He finally shifted to face her. "We will?"

"That's right," she said. "Or are you going to try to tell me there is no 'we'?"

He just looked at her for a moment. "No," he finally murmured, the sound of it vibrating through her. "I'm pretty sure there is a 'we.'"

Even as he said it, he was lifting his hand to her face. He stroked his thumb over the line of her cheekbone, his eyes poring over her with searing intensity, and she nearly trembled in response.

Then he stopped, something flickering across his face, and said roughly, "What if we can't?"

She frowned, not understanding. "What do you mean?"

"What if we can't figure it out?"

"We will," she said firmly, with no hesitation.

"But what if we can't?" he said, his tone deadly serious. "What if he gets away with it? Would you blame me?"

"Of course not," she said immediately. "I know you're doing everything you can. We both are. Whatever happens, I can't ask for more than that. I certainly wouldn't hold you responsible."

He exhaled slowly, and she had the sense that something had changed in that moment, though she didn't understand what. She didn't know why he would ask, why he would think she'd blame him.

His gaze gentled, a new tenderness in his eyes as they scanned over her face. "The first time I saw you I thought you were unbelievably beautiful," he said softly. "I kept waiting for that to change, to realize you weren't as beautiful as I thought you were that first moment. You couldn't be. But you are. I still almost can't believe it, but you are."

The wholly unexpected compliment brought a rush of heat to her cheeks. A chuckle worked its way from her throat. "Yes, well, the first time I saw you I thought you were the best thing I'd seen in a very long time."

It was his turn to laugh. "And that's changed?"

"No," she whispered. "Not at all."

"I'm glad to hear it," he said, his voice a low rumble. His smile deepened, and he suddenly, finally, drew her to him and kissed her.

There was no slow-building momentum this time. The first kiss quickly turned into another, then another, each faster, more urgent than the last. His fervor caught her off-guard at first, the raw hunger in his kisses more than she'd expected. Then something inside her responded in kind, the same eagerness, the same basic, elemental need surging within her. She caught up quickly, matching him kiss for kiss, their mouths meeting faster, harder. Each stroke of their tongues, each touch of their lips wasn't enough, only stoking the fire within her, making her want more.

It seemed as though whatever restraint had been keeping them in check had finally been stripped away, and there was nothing to stop them from what they both wanted. She didn't even think to question whether they should be doing this, whether it was too soon. If anything, it had been delayed too long, something that clearly had been building between them from the first moment they'd met. She couldn't think, couldn't worry about anything. She could only feel, only want, this man, this moment, more than she'd wanted anything in her entire life.

She placed her hands on his sides, only to once again encounter his coat. This time she didn't let it stop her, grabbing the lapels and pushing them back. He responded immediately, lowering his hands to grasp the front of the coat and pull it off. He let it fall to the floor, then reached for her again, his hands going around her back. Hers went to his chest, his arms. She smoothed her fingers and palms over the fabric of his shirt, felt his muscles tense beneath it, even as a groan of frustration rose in her throat. The coat was off, but it still wasn't enough. She needed his skin against hers, to feel the heat of him beneath her hands.

Before she could act, he was tugging at the bottom of her sweater. She helped him work it over her head, watched as he tossed it aside. Then he was reaching for her bra. In a deft motion, he released the clasp, then peeled the straps from her shoulders. Her breasts fell free, feeling impossibly heavy. They ached for his touch, and she thought he would do it, move his hands to her breasts once the bra was disposed with, take them fully into his palms.

Instead, he stepped back, holding her at arms' length. "I need to look at you," he murmured, his voice taut and thin, sounding as though he'd barely managed to force the words out. For a moment, he simply surveyed her, his eyes scanning over her. Her nipples tightened further, in the chill of the room, under his scrutiny.

Then he fell to one knee, his fingers finding the button on her pants and freeing it. She let him slide the slacks down her legs and stepped out of them, leaving her only in her panties. He pulled the pants free of her feet, his gaze slowly tracking up her legs. When they reached the apex of her thighs, now covered merely by a wisp of cloth that seemed as though it might as well be nothing, they stopped. A jolt shot through her, starting right there.

Without warning, he rose and swept her off her feet, his arms going under her knees and around her back. He carried her to the couch, then stopped abruptly. She glanced down and saw what he did, her laptop and notebooks and a multitude of papers spread on the cushions where she'd been working. Scrambling for a solution, she was about to suggest they go upstairs, even if she didn't want to wait that long, even if she didn't think they'd really make it.

He found an answer first, carefully lowering her to the floor and laying her on the plush rug in front of the coffee table, dropping on his knees beside her.

Propping herself on her elbows, she watched as he tore off his shirt, letting it fly to the side. The T-shirt beneath immediately followed, finally baring his torso to her.

She didn't have time to take in the view. As soon as the T-shirt was off, he lunged forward again, pushing her legs apart and moving between them. Reaching forward, he hooked his fingers into the waistband of her panties. She immediately raised her hips to let him drag them down her body. His fingernails scraped lightly against the soft skin of her hips, her thighs, as he slowly pulled the garment down her legs. Her eyes never left his, and his never left her body, studying her with a blatant intensity that made her insides shudder. She should have felt self-conscious, to lie totally naked in front of him, to have him center his interest on her bare body with such unyielding focus, his gaze stroking over her as tangibly as a physical caress. But she didn't. His eyes were too reverent, the expression on his face too purely appreciative of everything he saw, that she felt only pleasure at his attention.

She barely noticed when her underwear was off completely, didn't even see what he did with them.

"You are so beautiful," he murmured, his voice thick and rough. He didn't have to say the words. She saw them in his eyes and knew he meant every one.

Then he was sliding over her, his body massive, his strength surrounding her. She fell back against the rug as he moved upward. He finally stopped at her neck, bracing himself over her, and buried his mouth on her throat. The rest of their bodies weren't touching. It didn't matter. She could feel the heat of him radiating toward her from his arms, his chest, warming her skin as effectively as if they were pressed together. She lifted her hands, drawn to that heat and the bare skin she'd wanted to touch all this time and finally could. She trailed her fingers along his sides. His firm, smooth skin was as hot to the touch as she'd known it would be. She savored the feel of him, his tongue licking, his mouth sucking lightly at the sensitive skin at her throat, his own skin warm and muscled beneath her hands.

With one last kiss against her neck, he

shifted lower, forcing her to move her hands upward to his shoulders, tracing the endless width of them. He cupped her right breast in his palm, rolling his thumb over the soft roundness, then scraping over the engorged tip of her nipple. The sensation sent another rumble through her, and she shuddered under the force of it. Leaning forward, he copied the motion with his tongue, licking in small half-circles along the curve of her breast, finally reaching her nipple. He drew it into his mouth fully, sucking it against his teeth, then tracing its outline with the very tip of his tongue.

Adrift in sensation, she didn't know how long he continued, working one breast then the other. Eventually, he moved lower, slowly kissing his way down her body, as though he wanted to cherish every inch. And that was exactly how she felt, she thought faintly. Cherished. Adored as a result of his careful attention, his tender ministrations.

Then he reached her pelvis, the anticipation racing through her at what he might do next. Cupping her hips in his hands, he brought her up to his mouth, the heat of his breath against her center sending fresh waves of tremors through her even before his lips landed. Then his mouth was there, hot and insistent at the apex of her body. She gasped as his tongue darted out to tease her opening, probing gently, unerringly finding its way. She nearly squirmed in his hold, but his hands held fast, keeping her in place. Her eyes rolled back, her lids drifting shut as he worked with excruciating thoroughness, tasting her, licking inside her, pushing her higher and higher toward a release she tried to hold back as long as she could.

He must have recognized how close she was. Suddenly, with a low growl she felt against her core, he pulled his head away. Even as she registered the loss, she didn't feel its full impact, the sensations rolling through her so overpowering they continued long after the action that had caused them was removed. As if in a haze, she opened her eyes drowsily and peered down at him.

He shoved out of his pants, then fumbled with them. She didn't bother to look to see what he was doing. She looked only at him. This was the first chance she'd had to really do so, and what she saw sent a new rush of heat burning through her. His body was every bit as beautiful as she'd known it would be. His dark skin gleamed in the light of the room. His shoulders were broad, his arms and chest packed and muscular, his abdominal muscles clearly defined, the ridges firm and thick on his belly. And below them…She gazed at the evidence of his arousal, hard as stone, sticking up straight from his body. As she watched, it pulsed, bobbing slightly in the air. The sight gave her a thrill of pure satisfaction. *She* had that effect on him. He was responding that way because of *her*.

There was a brief tearing sound, then his hands moved to his erection and she saw he was covering himself. The sight of his fingers sliding over his shaft only fueled the ache inside her. She wished it was her fingers glancing over him, as much as she wanted him inside her, even as there was something incredibly sensual about seeing his own hands there.

The condom had barely hit the base of his shaft when he moved forward, sliding between her parted legs then over her, covering her with the length of his body once more. He stopped when they were face to face, bracing himself on his forearm. She felt the tip of his arousal against her folds, positioning itself there, prodding gently.

He dipped his head and lowered his mouth to hers. "Are you ready?" he whispered against her lips.

"Yes," she managed to say, the word not beginning to express how ready she was.

As soon as it left her mouth he thrust into her. She was already so wet and ready for him that one long, smooth stroke was all it took to bury himself in her to the hilt. The breath caught in her throat, just for a second, at the shock of his invasion. But it was more than that. From the sight of him, she'd known he would be big and thick inside her. He felt even more so. What she hadn't been prepared for was the sense of rightness, of how simply perfect this felt, having him there. Staring up into his eyes, she knew he'd felt it, too. She watched those eyes widen slightly, right at that moment of fulfillment. For the longest moment, he remained there, unmoving, simply filling her. Then he dropped his mouth to hers and kissed her again, long and hard, claiming her mouth as fully as the rest of her.

She tightened her muscles around him, driving a rough groan from his throat. He finally pushed his hips back, sliding out with agonizing slowness, then plunged in again, faster, harder. Again, she drew him in further, wanting him deeper, wanting everything she could get. She wrapped her arms around him and held him to her. They quickly built a rhythm, as he drove into her and she rose to meet each thrust. Through it all, they kissed, their mouths moving frantically, as fast as the movements lower between their bodies.

She struggled to absorb the feelings, the impressions, washing over her, not wanting to forget, to miss, a single one. Their tongues moving together, their lips meeting and clashing, the sounds of their soft moans being swallowed by each other's mouths. The muscles of his back rippling and shifting beneath her arms. The feel of his thrusts, their hips joining over and over again. The pressure building low in her body, growing more intense by the moment, pushing higher and higher inside her.

And most of all, that sense of rightness, unlike anything she'd ever known or thought could be. Even when the rush of her release finally swept through her, the tensing of his body above her saying he was right there with her, the feeling remained.

This was right. This was perfect. Because of this man, something she'd instinctively known from the first moment she'd seen him.

And nothing would ever be the same again.

Chapter Twelve

Lying in bed the next morning, Marcus smiled. He felt too good to do anything else, the feeling of contentment in his chest spreading outward to every part of his body. Staring at the ceiling, he wondered idly if he'd ever woken up feeling this happy. He doubted it. Because until this morning, he'd never woken up with Regina.

She was curled up against his side, fitting against him like she belonged there. Which she did, a purely primal instinct responded deep inside him, making him tighten his arm around her, drawing her closer. She cuddled against him in her sleep, her cheek on his chest, her soft fingers splayed over his belly, her warm breath wafting over his bare skin. He lowered his head and breathed in the scent of her hair, the scent of *her,* unable to get enough.

They'd managed to make it to her bedroom

sometime in the night, after lingering on the living room floor far longer than he would have thought comfortable, then taking a brief rest to satisfy other hungers in the kitchen, where they'd also lingered longer than expected. And yet, for everything they'd experienced downstairs and in this bed, he took a special pleasure from this moment, simply lying here with her, feeling this amazing woman beside him.

I certainly wouldn't hold you responsible.

Her words continued to stay with him, echoing through his mind. She'd said them with absolute certainty and no hesitation. The faith she'd shown in him had told him everything he needed to know about her and finally shown him the truth about his own judgments.

I know you're doing everything you can. We both are. Whatever happens, I can't ask for more than that.

If she couldn't, then how could he? Both of them, each in their own way, were fighting for some kind of justice in this world. But it wasn't a perfect world. He was only one man, and she was only one woman, both part of a larger system. They could each only do the best they could. Sometimes, no matter how hard they tried and despite their best intentions, justice may not be served. He couldn't hold her responsible for that. It didn't have to impact what was between the two of them, the way he felt about her. Maybe he didn't have to agree with every choice she made and everything she did, every client she took and every result that followed, any more than he could expect her to always agree with him. He just had to believe in her, the way she did in him, and believe that whatever she did was because she thought it was the right thing and the system was better off with her as a part of it.

And he did believe in her. Despite the short time he'd known her, he felt instinctively he knew the kind of person she was. Principled. Passionate. Someone who fought for what she believed in and those she felt worthy. He'd like to think it was something he'd recognized in her, part of what had drawn him to her from the start.

Whatever happened between them in the future, he knew better than to think it was going to be easy. Polinsky had already demonstrated that some cops were never going to like her. But he could deal with that. He didn't care about Polinsky's opinion or anyone else's. He only cared about his, and he liked this woman, more than he could remember liking any woman before, especially in such a short time.

She finally began to stir. Her body rubbed against him, her hand sliding over his abdomen in a feather-light caress, stoking an arousal that seemed like it had only just started to fade. He glanced down to see her eyes beginning to flutter, the sight making his heartbeat pick up speed in readiness. Moments later, she opened them fully and looked straight into his, sending a jolt through him. Her mouth curved in a lazy, utterly sexy smile, and he could only smile, too.

"Good morning," she said sleepily. He watched her lips form the words and suddenly he had to taste them again.

He bent his head and kissed her softly, just a quick connection, an appetizer to tide him over.

"Yes," he said. "It is a good morning."

And he kissed her again.

"SOMETHING'S BOTHERING ME."

Regina replaced the coffee pot on the machine and turned away from the counter. Marcus sat at the kitchen table, his brow furrowed in thought. "Really?" The smile that seemed to have been on her face from the moment she'd woken up deepened. "Nothing's bothering me."

He glanced up, his expression clearing, and matched her smile. "I meant with the case."

Of course. They'd taken too much time away from it already, she thought with a pang. Jeremy's killer was still out there, still on the verge of getting away with it. She wouldn't give up what they'd shared for anything, but it was time to get back to work. "What is it?" she asked.

"If Cole Madison is the father of Lauren's baby and doesn't want it coming out, why would he ask his father-in-law of all people to stop the investigation?"

"He wouldn't," Regina said, picking up his obvious train of thought. "He wouldn't want to raise Gaines's suspicions. I could see Tracy asking her father on her husband's behalf, but given the nature of our talk yesterday, I can't believe Madison would have told her about our visit, either."

"So realistically the only way Gaines could know that we even talked to Madison yesterday was because he found out on his own, which is possible since we were at his company. That means any actions he took were completely on his own, too. But why? From what we saw, he doesn't like the man. I can't really believe he would try to protect him."

"Especially if he has any suspicions about why we wanted to talk to Madison."

Marcus shook his head. "We're missing something."

She crossed to the table. "Well, as someone once told me, we could ask."

His mouth curved in a slow, irresistible grin. "Someone told you that, huh? Sounds like a pretty smart person to me."

"He's okay. Kind of full of himself."

He hooked an arm around her waist and pulled her to him, until they were face to face. "Oh, he is, is he?"

"Yeah, but it's all right. He has redeeming qualities, too."

"Really?" he said, his mouth achingly close to hers, his warm breath washing over her cheek. "I'd like to hear all about those."

"See? What'd I tell you? Full of himself."

"Guess I should put some of those redeeming qualities to work, then." He finally captured her mouth. It was a good thing his arm was around her. Her knees went weak the instant their lips met, heat rushing through her. She pressed her hands to his face, basking in the feel of his skin, his mouth on hers, his tongue sliding against hers, his arms around her. If she'd had any thought that last night might have gotten the feelings between them out of their systems, she would have been wrong. What they'd shared only seemed to have intensified the connection between them. She couldn't get enough. From the urgency of his hands on her back, his mouth on hers, neither could he.

The rational side of her knew it was probably crazy to be feeling such things when they'd only known each other such a short amount of time. The rest recognized that she'd never felt this innate closeness to another person, never responded nor felt such a deep recognition on a molecular level. The feeling was so heady she nearly felt giddy from it, not to mention his touch.

They finally broke the kiss, their breathing coming in fast, short pants. Neither tried to move more fully apart, remaining with their faces close. Her eyes pored over him, taking in the strong, sensual lines, the square jaw, the mouth still moist from hers. Her hands were still on his cheeks, framing his face. Some strange instinct wanted to hold on, as though she could capture this moment, this feeling, with this man and never let it go. Odd to think that she'd found him in the middle of such terrible circumstances, that something so awful could have brought them together.

The reminder brought back what they'd been discussing just moments before, what they really needed to be focused on now, she thought with an inner sigh, when all she wanted was to have her lips on his again.

"I guess I should have said *I* can ask," she said softly. "You can't talk to Gaines."

He arched a brow. "The hell I can't."

She finally dropped her hands and leaned back, the seriousness of the situation casting a pall on the closeness she'd been feeling. "What about your captain?"

"What about him? I'm too deep into this to turn back now. You had it right the first time. *We* can ask him."

Regina frowned. "Are you sure?"

"Don't tell me I'm going to have to convince you to let *me* come along now?"

"I don't want you to go if it means risking your career."

"Maybe my career doesn't mean as much if it comes with these strings."

"You don't mean that. I know how much your job means to you."

He sighed. "Yeah, it does. It's like you said, I became a cop for a reason. The big one was to make sure killers don't get away with murder. My job isn't more important than making sure Jeremy Decker's killer is caught."

She could tell he meant it. They weren't just words. And in spite of what they might ultimately mean, she couldn't help but feel a hint of pride at the strength of his convictions.

"All right," she said. "Let's talk to Gaines."

A CALL TO GAINES FINANCIAL informed them that Donald Gaines wasn't in the office today, which was probably to be expected since it was the final Friday before the holidays. Fortunately, they'd both already obtained the man's home address in Highland Park.

As she would have expected, the man lived in a veritable mini-mansion, a sprawling two-story building on a street with much of the same. Regina knew Gaines lived alone. His wife had passed away several years ago, and Tracy was his only child. One man hardly needed all that space, but, she supposed, the rich felt they had to keep up appearances.

Parking in the driveway, they made their way to the front door, where Regina rang the bell. A woman in a maid's uniform finally answered the door. "Can I help you?"

Regina stepped forward. Marcus's credentials weren't going to do them much good in this instance. Fortunately, she was more than willing to play as dirty as Gaines had when he'd called his friends. "Yes, my name is Regina Garrett. This is my associate, Marcus Waters, with the Chicago Police Department. I'd like to speak with Mr. Gaines."

"Is he expecting you?"

"No, he's not."

The maid's lips tightened slightly with disapproval, but she simply offered a bland "One moment please," and closed the door.

"You know she's going to come back and say he's unavailable, right?" Marcus asked mildly.

"I do. And you know I'm not going to take that for an answer, don't you?"

"I do," he said with a touch of amusement.

A minute later the door swung open again. "I'm sorry," the maid said, a noticeable lack of genuine apology in the words. "Mr. Gaines is not available to speak with you."

"I'm sorry," Regina returned just as coolly. "That won't work for me. I need to see him immediately."

"I'm afraid that won't be possible."

"Please inform Mr. Gaines that unless he wants his family's personal business exposed in the press, he'll make himself available. I presume he's in?"

The woman's jaw dropped in outrage. "I will tell him no such thing."

"Do you really think he'll appreciate you not giving him that message? Because I promise you, I'm not bluffing."

The woman stared at her for a long moment, mouth agape. Regina never blinked. The woman must have read just how serious she was, because she closed her mouth and raised her chin. "One moment," she said stiffly, no doubt trying to maintain her dignity in the face of such rudeness. Too bad Regina was beyond being concerned about being rude.

The maid closed the door again. It took her slightly longer to return, but Regina never doubted that she would.

When she finally opened the door again, her tense expression told Regina what the answer was before she gave it. "Right this way," the maid said, stepping aside and holding the door open fully.

"Thank you," Regina said with exaggerated politeness. She and Marcus stepped inside. As soon as they had, the maid shut the door and started down a hallway to the left, leaving them to follow.

They finally arrived at a closed door. The

maid knocked once, was greeted with a faint "Enter" and opened the door. Looking rather pointedly away, she held it for them.

The room appeared to be a library or some kind of home office. Massive shelves packed with books lined the walls, along with mounted animal heads and various trophies. It was very much a rich man's domain. Donald Gaines himself sat behind a massive desk, leaning back in an oversized chair as they entered. Regina moved briskly toward the desk without hesitating, not about to let the man feel at all like he had the upper hand even in his own territory.

"I don't appreciate being blackmailed, Ms. Garrett," he said, his voice thick with contempt.

"I don't appreciate people using their connections to obstruct police investigations, Mr. Gaines," she retorted, coming up to the desk. "At least what *I* did wasn't illegal."

"I'm sure I have no idea what you're talking about."

"So you didn't contact your friends in the police department to have them put an end to Detective Waters's investigation into your family's connection to Jeremy Decker?"

The man shot Marcus a withering glance.

"If that were the case, then Detective Waters has no reason to be here."

"I'm not." Marcus smiled slowly. "At least not in any official capacity. I'm simply here as an observer to support Ms. Garrett."

"And you don't have enough friends to get *me* to back off, Mr. Gaines. Now, I'd like to know why you attempted to use your influence to stall the investigation."

The man simply glared at her, every inch the king upon his throne. "Even if I did such a thing, why on earth would I tell you?"

She ignored the question. "The most logical conclusion is that you don't want Jeremy Decker's murder to be solved because you believe someone within your family is responsible."

"No, Ms. Garrett. The most logical conclusion is that I don't like to see my family harassed for no reason. As your presence here demonstrates, I'm rather protective toward my family. I don't care for the idea of their private business being raked over in the press, nor the idea of them being harassed by police officers on fishing expeditions with no basis."

"Asking relevant questions hardly counts as harassment, and I think we both know there is a basis. You know that Cole is likely the father of Lauren Decker's child, don't you?"

The man showed no surprise or outrage, which Regina figured was as good as a confirmation. He simply glowered at her, eyes narrowing to slits. "That's nothing but ridiculous conjecture, like most of what you and Detective Waters have been throwing around the past few days. Frankly, I've had enough of it."

"I was under the impression you don't like your son-in-law much." Regina continued as if he hadn't spoken. "Revealing his infidelity would be the perfect way to get him out of your daughter's life, wouldn't it?"

"You may have known how to talk your way into my house, Ms. Garrett, but don't presume you know anything about me or my feelings regarding my son-in-law. I am, above all else, a father, and I most certainly would not do anything to intentionally cause my daughter pain."

"Isn't it causing her pain to let her remain married to an unfaithful spouse and risk having her find out on her own?"

"We make the best decisions we can with the facts available to us. I'm comfortable with the choices I've made. I couldn't be less interested in whether or not you approve."

"Just how far are you willing to go to protect her from experiencing pain? Far enough to let her stay married to a killer, or enough to have someone killed yourself?"

"I'm sure I have no idea what you mean."

"Lauren Decker's brother Jeremy was murdered. The killer cut out his tongue, a pretty clear message they didn't want him talking about something. It's reasonable to believe that the paternity of Lauren's baby is what they didn't want him to reveal. The person most likely to be responsible would be the father himself. Or maybe someone else who doesn't want the father's wife to find out?"

Regina watched his reaction closely. If he was disturbed by the idea that his daughter was married to a murderer, or the suggestion that he himself was one, he didn't show it. He simply stared at her, stone-faced, as though she hadn't spoken at all.

"Ms. Garrett, I believe we're wasting each other's time. The reason I agreed to see you was to make it clear that I will not tolerate having my family's names tarnished in the media. I doubt you could actually get anyone in the press to spread these unfounded stories, but if you somehow do, I will hold you personally responsible. Rest assured, I will pursue all legal avenues against you, Detective Waters, and anyone else who spreads these lies."

She simply smiled. "As you probably know,

Mr. Gaines, I'm a defense attorney. In cases of libel, the best defense is the truth. First you'd have to prove they're lies. I don't think you can do that, can you?"

He didn't seem to have a quick comeback for that. He scowled at her for a long moment before finally saying, "I think we're done here."

She nodded once. "On that we agree."

Regina doubted he was going to offer her a proper goodbye any more than she planned to do the same. She simply spun on her heel and strode back to the door, Marcus falling into step beside her.

The maid was nowhere in sight as they made their exit. Regina still waited to speak until they were on the other side of the front door.

"What do you think?" Regina asked under her breath.

"I think I'm glad I never had to face you in a courtroom."

She smiled. "Besides that."

"I'm still looking for an answer to the question that brought us here, now even more since we've talked to him. He wasn't even caught off-guard by the idea that Madison fathered Lauren's baby. He definitely already knew. So why wouldn't he have told Tracy, why try to cover for Madison by stopping the investigation? I don't buy that he wouldn't want Tracy to know about her husband's affair to save her the pain of finding out."

"And did you notice he seemed completely unbothered by the idea that his daughter was married to a murderer? He has a good poker face, but even so, he didn't react at all."

"Which could mean he doesn't believe Cole is responsible for Jeremy's death. Because he himself is?"

"Or he has reason to believe there's another explanation altogether."

"A reason that either has to do with him or Tracy," Marcus said. "Or both. We need more information. I haven't had a chance to look into their backgrounds."

"I did," she said, already pulling out her cell phone. "My investigator did background checks on each of the Madisons when I took Jeremy's case, and I asked her to dig deeper a couple days ago when this all started. I read through what she sent me yesterday and nothing jumped out at me. Let's see if she has anything new for me."

SHE DIDN'T, BUT SAID she thought she was on to something and would call back shortly.

They returned to Regina's house to wait and regroup.

Two hours later Lynn finally called back. As soon as Regina heard what she had to say, she knew it was what they'd been looking for.

"Now, this is interesting," she said after ending the call.

Marcus was watching her from the other end of the couch. "What is it?"

"Tracy Madison was involved in an incident in her college days. No charges were filed and it seems her father paid for the damage—and more—but evidently she dumped gasoline in another girl's convertible and set it on fire."

Marcus frowned. "Why?"

"It seems Tracy found out her boyfriend slept with the girl and wanted some payback."

"She did say she didn't respond well to people taking her things."

"And that was just a boyfriend. You have to wonder how she'd react to another woman sleeping with her husband."

"I have a feeling that's what Gaines is doing. That's why he's trying to keep her from finding out about the affair."

"Or he's worried she already knows," she suggested. "That could be why he wasn't fazed by the idea that Madison was a killer or he himself could be suspected."

"Because if she knows, there's a chance she wouldn't have taken it out on her husband. She would take it out on the other woman. But why kill Jeremy Decker?"

"To limit the number of people who know and the chances of it getting out? It's one thing to have your boyfriend cheat on you. But your husband? That's much more humiliating."

"I guess there's only one way to find out." Regina grinned. "We ask?"

"Like a wise man once said."

"Wow. He's gone from a smart man to a wise man in just a few short hours. At this rate, I'm not sure I'll be able to keep up."

He laughed. "After that show you put on with Gaines, I really don't think that's going to be a problem. I'm pretty sure I'm the one who's going to be kept on my toes."

"And you're okay with that?" she asked curiously. She knew some men wouldn't be. A lot of men didn't want to be challenged. They wanted easy, undemanding women, wanted to feel smarter, as though their masculinity was wrapped up in the ability to feel superior to a woman. She didn't think he was like that. But more than that, she didn't want him to be.

"Sure. A truly wise man wouldn't want anything else, right?"

He grinned as he said it, the sight dazzling, the combination of the words and his smile utterly irresistible.

And if there'd been any question about it before, in that moment, she knew without a doubt that she was falling for this man.

Chapter Thirteen

The Madisons' home was an impressive two-story structure in Lincoln Park, but unlike at Gaines's house, it wasn't a maid who answered the door. Instead, Cole Madison responded to the doorbell himself, his expression hardening into a scowl at the sight of Marcus and Regina on his front step. "You again."

"May we come in, Mr. Madison?" Marcus asked with excruciating politeness.

"No," the man said immediately.

"Please, Mr. Madison. Is this really a conversation you'd like to have on your front step where anyone can overhear?"

"I don't intend to have it at all," he said. His arm tensed, no doubt on the verge of slamming the door shut.

"Then I guess we'll have to ask some of your neighbors about your wife—"

"Get in here," Madison said through

clenched teeth, yanking the door open and stepping aside.

Marcus let Regina enter first, then followed her in. Madison slammed the door shut and whirled to face them. "What do you want?"

"Don't worry, Mr. Madison. We're not here to see you. Like I was about to say, we'd like to speak with your wife."

"She's not home."

"Do you know when she'll be back?"

"She didn't say. What do you want to speak with her about?"

"Lauren Decker."

"You're out of your mind if you think I'm going to let you spread your lies to my wife."

"Spare us the fake outrage, Mr. Madison. We all know they're not lies, and Ms. Garrett and I are pretty sure your wife already knows. We're just here to confirm it."

Madison's brow furrowed. "What are you talking about? Knows what?"

"About your affair with Lauren Decker," Marcus said slowly, as if he was talking to a child. "That you're the father of her child."

Madison blinked at him in disbelief. "How could she know…something that isn't true?" he regained himself at the last moment.

Marcus decided to change tactics. "Do you

know your father-in-law tried to call in some favors to get me to stop investigating you in connection to Jeremy Decker's murder?"

The man's obvious confusion was answer enough. "No. I had no idea."

"Now does that sound like something he would do for you?"

Madison exhaled sharply. "No," he said flatly. "No, it doesn't."

"So you have to ask yourself, who would he do that for, and why? Maybe because he knows something? And if he knows something, who else do you think might?"

Frowning, the man stared blankly in front of him, his eyes unfocused. Marcus could practically see the thoughts racing through his head.

He was about to prompt the man when Madison suddenly turned and started out of the entryway.

"Mr. Madison—" Marcus called. The man didn't stop, didn't look back, didn't say a word. Seconds later he disappeared down the hallway.

Marcus lurched into motion, going after the man. He sensed Regina moving with him.

The doors along the corridor were open. A light shone from the one halfway down the hall on the right side, the only one that did. Marcus automatically headed toward it.

He stopped in the doorway, Regina coming to a halt just behind him. It appeared to be an office—a woman's, based on the furnishings. Tracy Madison's no doubt. Cole stood behind the desk, several drawers open in front of him. He appeared to have pulled some papers from the top drawer and was staring at them in disbelief.

"She knows," he said numbly. "She's known all this time and she didn't say anything."

Marcus stepped into the room. "What do you mean, Mr. Madison?"

After a beat, Madison held out the sheets of paper in his hand. "This is her office," he confirmed numbly. "I never come in here, never had a reason to. It's her private space. God knows, I don't want her poking around in mine…."

Marcus took the papers he offered, holding them so Regina could see them, too. They appeared to be handwritten notes penned by a woman. Lauren Decker's name immediately jumped out at him, along with the name of the restaurant where she'd met Madison, her phone number and address. Other sheets contained what appeared to be an investigator's report, containing a full background check.

There was really only one reason for Tracy Madison to know Lauren Decker's name and have gone to the trouble of obtaining this information, as Cole had already concluded. He and Regina had been right.

"So you admit you fathered Lauren Decker's child?" Marcus said, needing the man to confirm what they'd only been able to guess.

"Guess there's no point denying it now," he said softly. "If Tracy knows, then it's all over." He shook his head. "I knew she'd been secretive the past few weeks, and then this morning she said she had some things to take care of. I thought she was talking about Christmas stuff. She probably has a divorce lawyer by now. Hell, I suppose I need one of those now, too."

"That may not be the only kind of attorney you need, Mr. Madison," Marcus said.

It seemed to take a few seconds for the words to break through. Madison lifted his head and met Marcus's eyes. "What do you mean?"

"Tell me about Jeremy Decker."

"What about him?"

"Did you have anything to do with his death?"

"No! Why would I?"

"To keep him from revealing that you were the father of his sister's baby?"

"I never met or spoke with Jeremy Decker. I had no reason to believe he had any intention of revealing anything."

"So he never contacted you on his sister's behalf?"

"No. I only heard from Lauren. A few weeks ago she sent me a letter with a picture of the kid, telling me she was back in Chicago and needed help. Said she wanted to talk to me."

"And did you talk to her?"

"No. I didn't want to have anything to do with her."

"So you had Adrian Moore, someone who was capable of intimidating her, contact her on your behalf," Marcus guessed.

Madison nodded tersely.

"What did she want from you?"

"Money. For the *baby*," he finished on a sneer. Marcus could barely hold back his contempt at the way the man referred to his own child.

"You had to know this was only the beginning. As long as she had your child she had a reason to keep coming back for more."

Madison snorted. "Oh, believe me, I know."

"Maybe you didn't feel like paying. Maybe you or your man figured it would be easier to get rid of everybody who knew, and when you thought her brother might talk to his lawyer, if he hadn't already, you had to keep him quiet before more people found out or any paperwork was filed."

Madison glared at him. "Except by Tuesday, I was already working on getting the money, and I have the records to prove it. I just needed a few days to get it all in a way no one would notice. She knew I was working on it, so there was no reason for them to file any paperwork or tell anyone else. Moore finally told her on Wednesday that she'd have it by Friday. That's why he went to her house that day. You can ask her. Moore was supposed to deliver it today. She should have it by now."

Which explained why Lauren was ready to leave town. He'd agreed to give her the money. He was right. It did lessen his motive. But maybe not someone else's.

"Your wife never gave you any indication she suspected?"

"None."

"I wonder how she found out," Regina asked, drawing his attention back to her.

"I have no idea," Madison grumbled.

It was a good question. Had Madison

somehow let it slip, or was there another explanation? "Decker?" Marcus wondered out loud. Lauren could have told his wife long ago if she'd wanted, and it seemed unlikely she would have bothered now that she was on the verge of getting what she wanted. But a brother who didn't like how his sister was being treated? Maybe he'd decided Tracy Madison should know the truth about her husband, and had gotten more trouble than he'd expected as a result.

He saw from her expression she was thinking the same thing. "If so, what did she decide to do about it?" Regina asked.

Everything Madison had revealed seemed to have confirmed the suspicions that brought them here. They'd known that Tracy Madison had a history of not responding well to infidelity. Now they'd confirmed she knew about Madison's affair with Lauren Decker, and that she'd been secretive the past few weeks. What if Tracy Madison hadn't been busy finding a divorce lawyer? What if there was something else she intended to take care of? She wouldn't even have to do it herself. While she may have once set a rival's car on fire, she certainly had the money and resources to have someone else do her dirty work for her now. Even her father seemed to be concerned about the effect of having her learn such news.

Which meant Lauren Decker might be in danger.

"We should check on Lauren," Marcus said. Regina nodded immediately.

He started to move toward the door, then stopped and pulled out one of his business cards. "Mr. Madison, will you please call me when your wife gets home? I'd still very much like to speak with her." He figured it was a long shot at best that the man would call, but it couldn't hurt to ask.

After a moment Madison reached out to take the card, the corners of his mouth curling upward in the faint beginnings of a smile. "Absolutely," he said. "I'll be happy to."

Marcus read the malicious pleasure in the man's eyes, and it wasn't hard for him to figure out its cause. If Tracy Madison was planning to divorce her husband, he clearly intended to cause her as much trouble as she had in mind for him.

Nice people, Marcus thought grimly as he turned toward the door, more than ready to be done with the lot of them.

"YOU KNOW, I'VE NEVER understood the reasoning behind attacking the other woman,"

Regina said as Marcus drove them to Lauren's house. "If you're going to go after anybody when your boyfriend or husband cheats, why go after the other woman? Why not go after your boyfriend or husband? It doesn't make sense to me."

"That's because you'd never get that upset over a cheater. You'd just drop him and move on."

It had been a rhetorical question, so she was surprised by the seriousness of his answer. She looked at him curiously. "What makes you say that?"

"I just don't see you putting up with a man who doesn't deserve you. You've got too much respect for yourself for that."

He was right, of course. She had no use for liars, and she couldn't believe she'd ever waste her time with a faithless man. But she had to admit, having him recognize that about her and acknowledge it gave her a special pleasure.

Fifteen minutes later they reached Lauren's block. Regina had tried calling her, but the young woman hadn't answered. Her house seemed quiet and peaceful, if even more forlorn among the brightly lit homes that surrounded it. A faint light glowed through the curtains in the living room window. Regina hoped that was a good sign and Lauren was all right.

She still held her breath as they made their way to the door and knocked, then through the seemingly endless wait for someone to answer.

The door finally opened, and to Regina's relief, Lauren stood there, looking unharmed. She also looked no happier to see them than she had the day before. "What is it now?"

"Lauren, can we speak with you?" Marcus asked.

"I don't really have time. I'm trying to finish packing."

"So you really are leaving town?" Regina asked.

"First thing in the morning," she affirmed.

"It's almost Christmas. Are you sure you want to leave now?"

"I have to. There's nothing left for me here."

"This will only take a moment," Marcus said.

Not bothering to hide her impatience, Lauren grudgingly moved aside to let them enter. "Please keep it down. The baby's sleeping."

Regina and Marcus stepped inside. Lauren

closed the door behind them, then turned to face them, folding her arms over her chest, making no move to lead them into the living room. "What is it?"

"First we wanted to make sure you were okay," Marcus began.

Lauren waved a hand. "I'm fine."

"You haven't been threatened again? That isn't the reason you're so eager to leave?"

"I told you, there's nothing here for me anymore. I need a fresh start, for me and my baby."

"Lauren, I believe we're close to making an arrest in Jeremy's murder."

Her eyes widened slightly. "Who?"

"I can't say at the moment. But if we do make the arrest, we may need you to testify at the trial. For one thing, we may need you to talk about your relationship with Cole Madison."

"I told you—"

"Cole Madison already admitted it, Lauren," Regina said. "He told us he's the father of your baby and that he gave you money today."

Her expression hardened. "If he's saying I blackmailed him, he's lying."

Regina figured the young woman was an expert when it came to lying at this point, but wasn't about to say it. "He didn't say that. He admitted it was for the baby."

"That's right," Lauren said bitterly. "For the baby he didn't want."

Marcus suddenly reached for his cell phone. Checking the screen he said, "I have to take this," then took the call, raising the phone to his ear and stepping into the living room. Regina heard him murmur, "Waters" before he walked out of earshot.

Lauren's eyes tracked him as he left. Not wanting to waste any time she had with the young woman, Regina spoke again, drawing Lauren's attention back to her. "Lauren, are you sure you're not being threatened in some way? Because if you are, we will do everything we can to help you."

Lauren sighed, her exasperation clear. "It's nothing like that. I just can't stay here. It's too hard. There are too many memories."

"I understand. If there is a trial, it would still be helpful if you were willing to come back. Will you at least give us some idea where you're going? Maybe some way to reach you?"

"I'm not sure where I'm going. Guess I'll know when I get there."

Regina swallowed her impatience just as Marcus stepped back into the room. He looked at her. "Regina, can I speak with you for a moment?"

"Of course."

With a glance between the two of them, Lauren shook her head and threw her hands up. "Take your time. I have things to take care of." Moving past Regina, she stepped into what appeared to be the kitchen.

Marcus stepped close to Regina and lowered his voice. "Tracy Madison just returned home."

"Go," Regina said. "You should talk to her."

"What about you?"

"I'll stay here. I want to try to talk to Lauren more, get her to stay or at least tell me where she's going."

He hesitated. "You know, Lauren may still be in danger."

"She'll be fine. We know where Tracy Madison is, and she's nowhere near here."

"She could have hired someone to take care of the job for her."

"All the more reason for me to stay."

"If someone comes here, you're in no position to protect Lauren."

"Then she's certainly in no position to protect herself and her baby. If I'm here, at least she won't be alone. Safety in numbers, you know."

"I don't want you endangering yourself."

"And I don't want to leave a young woman and an innocent baby to fend for themselves. It's just a precaution. Most likely, nothing will happen and we'll all be fine. You need to go. If Tracy Madison is behind this, you have to make the arrest."

His eyes raked over her. He looked as if he wanted to argue with her. She knew he had no grounds to do so. What she said was completely logical.

The tightness of his expression said what he was feeling was anything but logical. By now she knew the feeling, and her heart melted a little. His only reason to object was concern for her, because he cared about what happened to her.

She saw the moment when he relented even before he began speaking. "Make sure that door is locked at all times while you're inside, monitor your surroundings at all times if you go out, and if you spot even the slightest hint of danger, get yourself and Lauren back in this house."

"Got it," she said.

"Stay safe," he murmured fiercely.

And even though she really didn't believe she was in any danger, she nodded, the words continuing to warm her long after he'd gone.

Chapter Fourteen

As Marcus approached the front door of the Madisons' home, the angry sound of raised voices met his ears. Coming closer, he was able to distinguish at least one male and one female speaker. Cole and Tracy Madison, no doubt, neither of them sounding very happy. He wondered what kind of situation he was entering, his hand automatically going to his weapon and resting there. He had no idea if he was going to need it, but given the sounds of the argument currently in progress, he didn't feel like taking any chances.

He rang the doorbell. The voices briefly fell silent, replaced by the tolling of the bell. Then the female voice picked up again, followed by the noise of footsteps stomping closer.

The door was flung open. Tracy Madison stood there, her face red, and gaped at him. "What are you doing here?"

"Your husband called and told me you were home."

"He did what?!" She spun around and stomped back into the house, leaving the door open. "You called a cop on me?"

"I guess you're not the only one who knows how to keep a secret!" Cole Madison's voice echoed from deeper in the house.

"Really? You're sleeping with half the sluts in this city and *I'm* the one keeping secrets?"

Marcus figured the open door was as much as an invitation as he could count on at this point. With a sigh, he eased his hand off his gun and stepped inside, closing the door behind him.

He followed the sound of the voices into the living room. Cole and Tracy Madison continued screaming at each other from opposite sides of the room. Some broken glass on the floor, apparently the remains of a vase judging from the flowers strewn across the carpet, indicated they'd already moved into the throwing-things phase.

Cole spotted him as he moved through the entryway. His face lit up. "Ah, Detective. So glad you could join us." He gestured extravagantly toward his wife. "Go ahead. Take her away!"

Tracy goggled at her husband as though he'd lost his mind. "What the hell are you talking about? Why would he take me away?"

"Because you're under arrest!" Cole crowed.

"For what?"

"Being a crazy bitch!"

Marcus felt a headache rapidly coming on. "Okay, that's enough," he said, raising his voice while trying to keep his tone cool. "Why don't we all calm down and just talk for a second? No yelling, no throwing things, just talking."

"Fine," Tracy Madison said through gritted teeth. "Perhaps you can explain what that bastard's talking about."

"Bastard, huh—" Cole started.

"Enough!" Marcus said, holding up a hand in the man's direction without looking at him. "*I'm* talking now." He focused his attention on Tracy Madison. "I'd like to speak with you about Lauren Decker."

At the mention of the name, Tracy shot her husband a glare, lips curling back in a sneer. "Well, she does seem to be the topic of the day."

"So you admit you know who she is?"

"You mean that she was my husband's

whore?" she scoffed in Cole's direction. "Yeah, I know."

"How long have you known?"

"Three weeks."

"How did you find out?"

"I came home early one day and overheard this idiot on his cell phone. He was talking to that creep Moore, telling him he had to handle Lauren and her baby, pay her off, get her to leave town."

"If you found out about this three weeks ago, why didn't you confront your husband?"

"I wanted to confirm what was going on and find out as much as I could before deciding what to do."

"Find out as much as you could about Lauren Decker?"

"That's right."

"And what did you decide to do with that information?"

"What do you mean?"

Cole interjected, "He wants to know if you're trying to kill Lauren, if you had her brother killed."

Tracy gaped at him, then at Marcus, the shock too real to be feigned. "What? Where'd you get that idea?"

"I recently learned about an incident in your past where you responded badly to an unfaithful boyfriend…." He let the comment trail off, leaving her to fill in the blank.

Tracy just blinked at him before comprehension fell over her. She threw her arms up. "Oh, come on! You set one car on fire and people hold it against you the rest of your life. I was twenty years old! It was years ago! One crazy moment doesn't mean you're crazy all the time."

"Except you *are* crazy," Cole said.

She whipped her head in his direction. "And you're a cheating bastard who's about to be broke and homeless. Enjoy having a roof over your head right now, because those days are numbered!"

"Enough!" Marcus yelled again, cutting off whatever Cole had been about to say. When the pair fell quiet, both seething silently and pointedly looking away from each other, he continued. "You're saying you haven't done anything to try and harm Lauren Decker or any member of her family?"

"No," she said petulantly. "I've matured since college."

Marcus figured it would be better if he didn't respond to that. Cole Madison didn't show as much restraint, the sound of his snort loud in the room.

To Marcus's surprise, Tracy ignored the

man. "Besides, why would I want to hurt her? She's the best way to hurt *him*." She jerked her head toward her husband.

"What do you mean?" Marcus asked.

"She just proves what an idiot he is, and soon the whole world is going to know it."

"What exactly are you talking about, Mrs. Madison?" he asked, quickly growing tired of her vagueness.

"I'm talking about my husband being too stupid to investigate Lauren Decker the way I did." Tracy smiled, her triumphant expression sending a warning through Marcus's system. "You see, Detective, this time, *I'm* not the crazy one."

REGINA STOOD RESTLESSLY IN Lauren Decker's living room, trying to figure out what to say to the young woman. Lauren had disappeared into the back of the house, saying she had things to pack. Regina had offered to help, hoping to be able to speak with her as they worked if necessary, but Lauren had said she didn't want to risk her waking the baby. At this point, Regina figured Lauren was just using her child as an excuse, but she couldn't exactly call her on it. God forbid she actually did wake the baby.

So she waited for the young woman to

return, or for the baby to wake up and remove Lauren's cause for objection. Hopefully the baby's naptime would be over soon.

In the meantime, everything was quiet. Not a single sound reached her ears. Fittingly enough given the season, it truly was a silent night. The house was completely silent. As it had been every other time Regina had visited the house. Completely, utterly silent.

It suddenly struck her how odd that was, and she frowned. In all the times she'd been in this house, she'd never so much as heard Lauren's baby make a sound. Lauren had always said the baby was asleep or napping, the way she had now. Regina was no expert when it came to babies, and she did know they slept a lot, but it was strange that Lauren's baby always seemed to be asleep no matter what time of day they'd been there and that Regina had never heard a peep from her.

Troubled, she glanced around the room. She noticed there were no pictures of the baby and couldn't remember ever seeing any. She guessed that made a certain amount of sense. Even if Lauren wanted to put up pictures of a baby she saw every moment of every day, she'd been home only a few weeks and probably hadn't had a chance.

But the absence of other things couldn't

be explained away as easily. With everyone she'd ever known who'd had a child, baby paraphernalia had seemed to be everywhere. Yet Regina realized she'd never seen any of that in this room, even before Lauren had started packing. No baby blankets, no toys, no used bottles or stray pacifiers. No crib or playpen, no stroller here or in the entryway for when Lauren took the baby out.

With increasing dread, Regina tried to think of a single baby-related item she'd seen in this house. A stray little sock. A package of diapers, or even a single loose diaper. She couldn't come up with anything. Of course, she'd never seen the baby herself. She was always in the other room.

Always sleeping. Always quiet.

Uneasy with where her thoughts were leading her, Regina tried to dismiss them. What she was thinking was crazy.

Wasn't it?

She suddenly heard Lauren in the hallway, moving nearer. From the sound of her footsteps, she'd moved into the kitchen.

Acting strictly on impulse, Regina called out, "Would it be all right if I used your bathroom?"

Lauren didn't answer at first, the hesitation lasting far too long for what should have been a simple question. Or was Regina reading something that wasn't there? "Sure," Lauren said finally, her voice muffled. "It's right down the hall. Just try to be quiet."

"Of course," Regina replied. For the baby. Another indication of an overprotective mother, or something else? "Thanks. I really appreciate it."

She stepped out into the hall. Lauren didn't reply, but Regina could hear her moving around in the kitchen, her steps light.

Regina suddenly felt a vibration in her bag. Her cell phone. She ignored it, cautiously moving forward down the hall, glancing behind herself every so often to make sure Lauren remained out of sight. She had to move quickly. She had to know.

The bathroom was the first door on her right. Reaching in, she quickly flipped the light on and pulled the door shut. It wasn't loud enough to wake any potentially sleeping babies, but enough that Lauren should be able to hear it if she was listening from the kitchen, and Regina didn't doubt she was. The only thing she wasn't sure of was the reason.

There were four doors left. One was smaller than the others, its proximity to the bathroom door and placement between it and the next telling her it couldn't possibly lead to a room.

She guessed it was a closet and moved on. That left three.

The next one had a light on in it. From the open boxes and feminine feel to the space, Regina figured this was Lauren's room. There was no sign of a crib or any baby gear in sight. That didn't necessarily mean anything. Lauren might not be the kind of mother who felt the need to keep her baby in the room with her. There might be a nursery.

The next room, its door adjacent to Lauren's, had a masculine vibe. There was enough childhood memorabilia to indicate a boy had once lived here, but also enough in the furnishings and spareness of the items to suggest that that boy had grown up. *Jeremy's room,* Regina thought with a pang. This had been Jeremy's room.

She didn't let herself linger. Pushing the wave of sadness aside, she moved on.

That left one. The door was almost directly across from the door to Lauren's room. Not a bad place for a nursery, Regina supposed.

The door was slightly ajar, and Regina could see the room inside was dark. Hoping it wouldn't make a sound, she pressed her hand against the door and slowly eased it open.

As she'd seen, the room was bathed in blackness. There wasn't a single light in the room—no nightlight, no outside light from the windows. The only illumination came from the hallway where she stood, the glow spilling into the room and over an object against the far wall.

It was a crib.

Part of her immediately felt foolish for her half-formed suspicions. Yet something compelled her to move forward. Without thinking, she stepped into the room, as though inexorably drawn to the piece of furniture.

She treaded carefully, the carpeted floor absorbing the sounds of her movements. The closer she came, the more her tension grew. She wasn't sure what she expected to find, didn't know what she wanted to find. She only knew that she had to know.

Then she was finally standing next to the crib. Leaning closer, she peered into it, narrowing her eyes against the darkness. She couldn't see much, only the vague shape of a blanket, its appearance too flat to be covering much beneath it.

Reaching down, she grabbed an edge and whipped the blanket off the surface.

There was nothing underneath it. The crib was empty.

There was no baby in this house. Regina suspected there never had been.

She sensed the movement behind her a heartbeat too late. She started to turn—

The heavy weight slammed directly into the side of her head, knocking her off-balance, blurring her vision. She threw her arms out, one to steady herself, the other to ward off another blow.

It didn't work. Pain exploded in her head again. She felt herself falling, landed on her side, barely registered the carpet beneath her.

Dazed, she tried to turn her head, tried to look up, tried to blink and clear her vision so she could see—

But all she saw was a dark shape flying toward her face before another blow struck her and stole every thought completely.

Chapter Fifteen

"Damn it."

It took everything Marcus had in him not to throw his phone out the window. Instead, he forced himself to simply disconnect the call and hit Redial to try again.

Regina wasn't answering, hadn't been for the past five minutes. Either she had her phone shut off or something was keeping her from taking the call.

It was the second possibility that had him slamming his foot down on the accelerator and weaving through traffic as much as was safe, all while working his phone with one hand and keeping it on speaker.

He'd radioed for a car to be sent to Lauren Decker's house, only to be told there was some kind of major accident in the area and all available officers had been dispatched. They would try to send someone ASAP, but at the rate he was going he suspected he'd get there first. He just didn't know what he'd find when he got there, a fact that scared the hell out of him.

Tracy Madison had indeed been busy the past few weeks—busy uncovering the truth about the woman who'd claimed to have had her husband's child. A child that there was no evidence even existed. Her investigator had tracked Lauren's movements between the time she first left Chicago and when she returned. No birth certificate had ever been filed anywhere, and though she'd been careful, he'd managed to find enough people who'd encountered her during that period to raise serious questions that she'd ever been pregnant at all.

A nonexistent child. That seemed like a secret worth killing over, especially to someone unhinged enough to try pulling it off in the first place.

If it was true, the woman had killed and mutilated her own brother.

Marcus didn't even want to think about what she was capable of doing to Regina.

Except he did think about it, unable to think about anything else as the terror climbed higher and higher inside him.

The idea of anything happening to her… He

never should have left her there, never should have left her alone.

If he found her safe and in one piece, he damn well never would again.

"Come on," he muttered as the buzz of each subsequent ring filled the car.

Finally the call kicked over to voice mail.

And there was nothing he could do but call again.

THE FEELING OF SOMETHING tugging at her legs pulled Regina back to consciousness. Her head throbbing, she slowly pried her eyes apart when all she wanted was to keep them closed. But she wanted whatever was yanking on her legs to stop even more.

Blearily she tried to move her arms, only to find they wouldn't. She looked down to see her wrists strapped together with duct tape, and farther down, Lauren wrapping the last of another roll around her ankles.

Instantly awake, Regina pulled her legs back to kick out—

Lauren lurched upward from the crouch she'd been in and glared down at her. "So you're awake," she grunted. "It would have been easier if you stayed knocked out, but you couldn't even do that for me, could you?"

"Sorry for making it harder for you to kill me," Regina scoffed.

Lauren shrugged and tossed the empty roll aside. "Doesn't matter. It'll get done one way or another. If you really want to apologize for something, you can start with everything else."

Regina gaped at her. "What are you talking about?"

"This is all your fault, you know. If you'd just left Jeremy in jail until after Christmas, none of this would have happened. I would be long gone, Jeremy would still be alive and we wouldn't be here right now."

"You killed your own brother," Regina said, the full implications hitting her. Horrified, she stared at the young woman. *"You cut out his tongue."*

Lauren stared back at her, no expression whatsoever on her face. "He was going to betray me. He was going to tell you, and as soon as he made that decision, he wasn't my brother anymore. Family doesn't betray you."

Both the flatness in her eyes and lack of emotion in her words sent a shiver of warning through Regina. If she couldn't already guess, it was clear the woman was seriously disturbed. Regina swallowed slowly, trying to think of a way out of this. There wasn't a doubt in her mind the woman was fully capable of killing her, might just be moments away from doing so. She had to keep her talking, had to figure out what to do. "Was there ever a baby?" she asked.

"There would have been," Lauren said with a trace of sadness, her eyes growing even more distant. "When I found out I was pregnant, I was so happy. I thought that was all it would take to get him to leave that rich bitch of a wife. But Cole wasn't happy. He screamed at me, told me to get rid of it, tried to give me money to pay for it. I loved him, you know? He was everything I ever wanted. I only wanted to be with him. So I did it. I got rid of it to make him happy so we could be together."

Her face hardened. "But when I tried to call him to tell him I'd done it, he wouldn't pick up. I didn't want to leave a message. I wanted to tell him personally so I could see and hear his reaction when he found out what I'd done for him, how much I loved him. But when somebody called me back, it wasn't Cole. It was that thug who works for him. 'Is it done?' That's what he asked me. I told him it was none of his damn business and I wanted to talk to Cole. He told me Cole didn't want to talk to me. He just wanted to know if I took care of it. Can you believe that? I got rid of my baby for him and he wouldn't even *see* me. And I knew if I told him I had he still wouldn't see me. So I told that creep I hadn't done it. And if Cole wanted to ask me anything, he would have to do it himself."

"Did he?"

Lauren snorted. "No. He just sent that thug after me, had him threaten me. And I knew I had to make him pay."

Regina subtly shifted her wrists to see how much give the tape had in it. A little, but not nearly enough. Still, she had to start somewhere. She kept talking to keep the woman's attention off her wrists. "Why didn't you tell his wife?"

"I wasn't telling that bitch anything," Lauren spat. "Besides, I wanted him to suffer. Telling her was too easy. It was much better to make him worry about her finding out than making it happen."

"So you broke into his house."

Her mouth twisted in a satisfied smirk. "I deserved that jewelry. I was going to leave a clue so he'd know it was me. But then Jeremy followed me and tried to stop me. I hadn't told him what I'd done—I knew he wouldn't approve. He barely found out I was pregnant when he went out and got that crib. He thought I was just angry that Cole wouldn't talk to me. But then he was arrested, and it all worked out. He never had to know. I left town for a while so Cole wouldn't know I hadn't had a baby, then I came back and sent him a picture of a baby so he'd know it was time to pay up. I knew he would. But then you got Jeremy out of jail, and that's when it all started to fall apart."

"Did you break into my office?"

"I wanted to know what you knew, especially after you kept coming here asking questions. I knew you weren't going to stop. It didn't seem like you knew anything, but I was worried Jeremy might have given you some hints and you just didn't realize it yet. I couldn't have you figuring it out. Turned out you didn't really know anything. Too bad you didn't stay that way."

"So what are you going to do now? You can't kill me. Detective Waters knows I'm here. If anything happens to me, he'll know you're responsible."

"Maybe. He just won't be able to prove it." Lauren reached down and picked up another roll of tape, slowly peeling a long piece without tearing it off. "We're going for a drive. Only one of us is coming back."

She started forward, and Regina realized the woman intended to tape her mouth shut so she couldn't make a sound when she dragged her to her car. If she pulled the car all the way to the back of the driveway, she might be able to pull it off without anyone seeing, especially with the house so dark and unlit. Which meant if Regina was going to make a sound, it was going to be now.

She threw her mouth open and screamed at the top of her lungs, as much to startle the woman as to possibly alert anyone outside what was happening. Lauren briefly cringed, turning her face away, but when she faced Regina again, her expression was only more determined. She started forward again.

A sudden pounding erupted on the front door. "Police! Open up!"

Marcus, Regina recognized, joy seizing her chest.

This time Lauren *was* startled. She jerked her head to the noise, eyes going wide, stumbling slightly.

Regina didn't hesitate. She pulled her legs back and kicked out, sending her feet straight into the woman's abdomen. With a screech, Lauren flew backward, her head slamming into the wall behind her with a dull thud. Her eyes dazed, she started to slide down the wall, the roll of tape still in her hand tumbling from her fingers.

Almost simultaneously, Regina heard the front door crash open, then footsteps pounding closer.

And then Marcus was there. He stopped in the doorway, eyes wide, glancing from the woman at his feet to Regina, bound on the floor. Swearing softly, he started toward Regina.

"No," she said, shaking her head firmly, then wincing at the pain that seared through her skull. "Deal with her first. She's crazy enough to snap out of it any second."

"My pleasure." Pulling out his handcuffs, he flipped the woman onto her stomach and yanked her arms behind her. She finally snapped out of her daze and started to struggle, screeching anew, curses flying. He relentlessly tightened the cuffs over her wrists, reciting her Miranda rights in a tone that didn't begin to hide the anger he was feeling. Only when he said the final words did he rise and turn away, leaving her flailing on the floor.

He quickly moved to Regina's side. Bending, he reached for her wrists, fingers fumbling at the tape. "So much for coming to the rescue," he murmured. "I should have known you would save yourself."

"Not quite," she smiled. "And I couldn't have done it without you. Thanks for the assist."

"Glad to help," he said, his voice thick, driving a lump to her own throat.

It took some effort, but he managed to loosen the end of the tape, then pulled it off in several fast, angry jerks. A sigh of relief worked from her lungs when the last of it was off and he tossed the balled-up strip aside.

She expected him to shift to her ankles to free them next. He didn't. Instead, he reached forward and pulled her into his arms. She could feel his heart pounding, the heavy thuds vibrating through her body. He seemed to surround her. At the feel of him, her shoulders dropped, the tension that had been clutching her rapidly fading. She wrapped her arms around him, holding him to her as much as he was her.

He didn't say anything. He didn't have to. She didn't speak, either. In the distance she heard approaching sirens. She barely noticed. All that mattered was his arms around her, his grip fierce and tight, as though he never intended to let her go.

Epilogue

Regina couldn't remember the last time she'd stayed up until midnight on Christmas Eve. For years, it had simply been another night for her, with no reason not to go to bed early, no reason to stay up late.

But then, this wasn't just any Christmas, and she was in no hurry to bring this evening to an end.

They lay on her living room couch, her back to his chest, Marcus's right arm slung loosely over her. They were sharing a blanket, but that wasn't what caused the warmth that seemed to fill every inch of her body. It was the simple perfection of this moment, of being here with him.

They'd turned off most of the lights, giving the room an even cozier feel. The only lights came from the Christmas tree across the room, the tiny multi-colored bulbs flickering on and off. The tree had been a surprise. She hadn't thought she needed one, already plenty in the holiday mood without one by then, but he had. She suspected it couldn't have been easy to find a decent-looking Christmas tree at such a late date, but somehow he'd managed it. They'd decorated it together with some random items he'd found, what was left in the stores at the end of the season. The decorations didn't really go together, but Regina didn't care. It was without a doubt the most beautiful tree she'd ever seen.

As though reading her thoughts, or simply looking at the same thing she was since it was directly in their line of sight, he murmured, "I have to say, I think we did a great job on that tree."

She smiled. "I think so, too."

"I just wish it didn't look so empty underneath. It might look better with some presents under it."

"It's perfect," she said firmly. "And I don't know what we could put under it. I already have everything I want."

And she did. Everything had worked out. Jeremy's murder had been solved and his killer brought to justice. Lauren Decker was in jail, and though she knew Jeremy wouldn't have taken any pleasure in his sister's fate,

Regina hoped the resolution had brought his spirit a measure of peace.

Marcus hadn't heard a word about the way he'd talked to Gaines and the Madisons after being ordered not to. It wasn't too surprising. Given how everything had turned out and what had been revealed, the parties involved had more important matters to think about. Tracy Madison had wasted no time kicking Cole out of the house and retaining a divorce attorney. She wasn't the only one looking to end a partnership. Marcus had requested a new partner, something Polinsky hadn't objected to. It sounded as if he would know something at the beginning of the year.

And meanwhile she was here, with him. No present could be better than what she had at this moment.

The realization filled her with a sense of wonder. It really was amazing. A week ago she'd resigned herself to spending Christmas alone, never imagining what would happen in the following days, what she would find.

A week, that voice in the back of her mind echoed suddenly, dampening the happiness inside her. She tried to brush the thought aside, but found that she couldn't. It was too insistent, bringing with it a whisper of uncertainty she couldn't quite silence.

She'd known him for such a short amount of time. Most people would think it was crazy to feel so strongly for a man she'd known less than a week. Normally she would be one of those people. She was thirty-five, long past the age when she should be capable of falling head over heels or being swept off her feet by someone she hadn't known all that long. She had too much sense to have it ever happen before.

And yet, here she was. Which either meant she had somehow become foolish without realizing it over the years, or too desperate to know better, or there was something more here, something real, despite how impossible that might seem.

She must have tensed without realizing it, because he suddenly asked, "What's wrong?"

Embarrassed, she almost denied it. But she'd never been afraid to speak her mind before. She wasn't going to start now. "I was just thinking about how fast this happened. Does that worry you at all? That we haven't known each other very long?"

"Why would it? If it's this good now, imagine how good it'll be when we've known each other longer."

His words sent a thrill through her. "You think it'll only get better?"

"I think it's worth investigating."

She smiled. "So you want to continue our partnership?"

"It's worked pretty well this far, don't you think?"

"I do."

"Then it wouldn't make much sense to quit when we're just getting started."

He was right. It wouldn't. And they *were* just beginning. She remembered that night when he'd first kissed her and she'd looked forward to what would happen next. She still did. What they had now was great, but she knew they could have so much more.

And they would. Suddenly, without a single doubt or hesitation, she knew that, too.

"Look at that," he said softly against her ear. "It's midnight."

She glanced at the clock, the hands briefly appearing in the flashes of light from the tree, and saw he was right. It was officially Christmas.

She turned in his arms, twisted her neck to see his face. Even in the faint, flickering glow of the Christmas lights, she saw him clearly. The beauty of his face. Its strength.

Its character. The way he gazed down at her, his eyes softened with tenderness.

He bent his head and kissed her, slowly, lovingly. When they broke apart, he continued to gaze at her steadily, that look never fading from his eyes.

He smiled. "Merry Christmas, Regina," he said softly.

"Merry Christmas, Marcus."

As he held her close and she felt the strength of his body wrapped around hers, she let the last of her doubts slip away. Maybe it was fast, maybe it was inexplicable, maybe it was hard to believe. But then, miracles usually were.

And she had no doubt there was something miraculous about this. Because she hadn't asked for this, hadn't made a wish list or asked for anything for Christmas in years. And yet, here he was, exactly what she wanted, for Christmas and for always.

A good man. A real man. A true man.

And he was all hers.

* * * * *

LARGER-PRINT BOOKS!

GET 2 FREE LARGER-PRINT NOVELS

PLUS 2 FREE GIFTS!

HARLEQUIN®

INTRIGUE®

Breathtaking Romantic Suspense

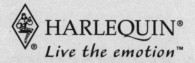

HARLEQUIN®
SuperRomance®

...there's more to the story!

Superromance.
A *big* satisfying read about unforgettable
characters. Each month we offer *six* very different
stories that range from family drama to adventure
and mystery, from highly emotional stories to
romantic comedies—and much more! Stories
about people you'll believe in and care about.
Stories too compelling to put down....

Our authors are among today's *best* romance
writers. You'll find familiar names and talented
newcomers. Many of them are award winners—
and you'll see why!

If you want the biggest and best
in romance fiction, you'll get it
from Superromance!

Exciting, Emotional, Unexpected...

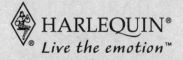

HARLEQUIN®
Live the emotion™

HARLEQUIN®
Presents

The world's bestselling romance series...
The series that brings you your favorite authors,
month after month:

Helen Bianchin...Emma Darcy
Lynne Graham...Penny Jordan
Miranda Lee...Sandra Marton
Anne Mather...Carole Mortimer
Melanie Milburne...Michelle Reid

and many more talented authors!

Wealthy, powerful, gorgeous men...
Women who have feelings just like your own...
The stories you love, set in exotic, glamorous locations...

HARLEQUIN®
Presents
Seduction and Passion Guaranteed!